Also by the author

Strawberry Moon
Cathead Bay
Providence Times Three
Death Of The Mystery Novel
Once Dead Long Dead
Suttons Bay

A DESPERATE RUSE

The Sherlock Holmes Case

ROBERT UNDERHILL

A DESPERATE RUSE

The Sherlock Holmes Case

ROBERT UNDERHILL

Northport, Michigan

Library of Congress Control Number 2014937212
Underhill, Robert

A Desperate Ruse / Robert Underhill - 1st. edition
p.cm
ISBN 13: 978-0-9798526-7-1
    1. Crime - Fiction 2. Sherlock Holmes 3. Psychiatry

Printed in the United States

My thanks to Barbara Abbot, Ed Dorsey, Tom Dunfee, Mike Fleishman and Kathleen Snedeker for their valuable help.

For those of Dr. John Watson's faithful readers, who sensed something was amiss.

London, Thursday, 3rd. February 1881

"He should have been here by now," said the stout distinguished looking man peering expectantly through the window onto Charles Street, his statement directed toward me. We were in the heavily-draped and richly-furnished drawing room of his Mayfair home. Contained in his declaration and the tension in his voice was concern for his younger brother, ostensibly my reason for being there. But I also began to be aware the man had another concern—his wish to survive in the competitive world of high office in Her Majesty's government. I was there in the role of his advisor, a seemingly improbable role given his great wealth, his high social position and the fact that I was half his age.

I was thirty-three, but looked younger, a fact I attempted to ameliorate by growing a beard and wearing my hair longer than the standard fashion, something I had picked up in the company of Viennese colleagues. I have reflexively assumed a maturely reserved manner in situations such as the present one, just as one tends to crouch in the presence of gunfire. I have been mistaken for a fledgling symphony conductor and once for an Italian count. The intricate embroidery of the muted waistcoat that I was wearing beneath a conservative, well-tailored suit would support either impression. Against the latter choice stood the evidence of my speech and habit of movement, which betrayed me as a product of a British public school.

I sat in what was probably an authentic Chippendale arm chair, near a burnished mahogany table upon which I had just set down a glass of a very good *fino* sherry.

"It looks like he's not coming. I'm sorry," the man at the window said with irritated resignation. "Apparently he has chosen to forgo collecting his 'packet', as he terms it. But see here, it's really my fault that you've wasted your time coming here. I of all people should know how unpredictable he's become." He paused in his pacing to stare searchingly out the window once more, looking up and down the length of the street. He slipped a gold watch from a vest pocket, glanced at it and replaced it in a well-practiced movement.

"It was only my desperate hope that I could get some help with this worsening situation that has caused me to believe this evening would be different."

"Don't trouble yourself, Mr. Holmes. I understand

completely," I assured him.

Taking a final glance out the window, he began to turn away, accepting the failure of the plan he had spoken of. He stopped abruptly and murmured, "Can it be?" He then declared, "Yes. He's crossing the road now. And, of course, the ragged news vendor who had been standing there on the opposite sidewalk is gone. How obtuse of me." He turned to face me at the table. "He is given lately to wearing disguises. I should have known. Dressed as a news peddler, he's been watching the house."

After saying this, he now left the window and strode across the broad Persian carpet to stand before me.

"As I suggested earlier, you'll be a colleague from the Ministry . . . secretary to the Assistant Councel—that is, if you don't mind."

"My pleasure."

My host tried to assume a conversational tone while at the same time speaking louder. "Ah yes, ah, Andrews, I'm much obliged to you for bringing those papers 'round in person this evening."

In the next instant, the door of the room opened and closed quickly. Now standing inside the door was a tall, lean man. The clothes he'd been wearing in his role as news vendor had been discarded, revealing a belted

Norfolk jacket of good workmanship. He held a book loosely to his chest with one hand. His face was striking. Every feature was angled in flat planes as if struck from a block of marble by single chisel strokes. Hawk eyes flicked quickly to the corner where I sat and then to the window where, at the end of several long, gliding strides, and after glancing furtively around the edge of the brown velvet drape at the street below, he closed the drapes completely. Calmly he walked to and dropped languidly into a chair. He poured himself a glass of sherry from the decanter on the writing desk next to the chair and then, in a deliberately unhurried and supercilious manner, said in a voice that was a high-pitched, yet perfect dramatic instrument, "Are you going to introduce your friend, brother?"

With an effort to match the offhand tone the newcomer had just affected, the stout man, said, "Yes . . . Yes, certainly. This is, ah, George Andrews. Andrews stopped by with some papers from the Assistant Councel."

Not hiding an ironic smile, the newly arrived man commented, his eyes making a mock dramatic sweep of the room, "That so? Tucked them neatly away already have you?"

Visibly off balance the stout man began, "Right. Yes, ah, .. Andrews, let me introduce my brother . . . "

"Let's not insult our guest, dear brother. I'm sure he already knows who I am, *nicht wahr, mein Herr?*"

This unexpected question caused me to hesitate a moment, then I smiled and said, "Very true, sir."

The lean man's smile broadened. "Andrews. George Andrews." He appeared to ponder. "George? Now I would have thought Georg to be more apt."

The older brother, showing physical signs of anxious discomfort, fidgeted and touched a handkerchief to his sweating forehead. I, on the other hand, was calmly enjoying the confrontation.

Calm also was the younger brother, stretching his long legs in front of him now, while crossing both arms over the book he was carrying. Quite suddenly he stood erect, advanced toward me and, stopping only a couple of paces away, looked down and began a rapid recitation, "If in the future you should have papers to deliver from the Ministry, I think, my dear Mr. George Andrews, you'll find the way is kinder to your boots if you were to hire a cab rather than walk out of your way through St. James Park, stopping at the duck pond. Otherwise, you will have to visit Salamander on your next trip to Vienna to replace them. No doubt you'll be making that journey soon to deliver recent photographs you've taken and developed of a certain new warship." His smile had become a knowing sarcasm. "All may not go as you plan, Mr. George Andrews. That, however, will have to wait. I have other matters to attend to tonight. I bid you both a good night."

He turned on his heel and in an instant was at a bookcase near the door. Here he placed the book he was carrying on a shelf, took a book from another shelf and moved quickly to the door, which he opened a crack to listen for a moment, then slipped through and was gone.

I was about to speak when my host raised a warning finger to his lips, then went to the bookcase and withdrew the book his brother had put there. From it he took a slip of paper and walking over to where I was seated, handed it to me. I looked down at two words written in flamboyant script: *Fishy Fish*.

"Fish . . ." I began to say.

Again the warning finger silenced me and he took back the slip of paper and motioned to be followed toward the door.

"And please convey my thanks to the Assistant Council for answering my request so promptly," he said loudly. He then opened the door, adding, "I'll show you out, Andrews."

ADDENDUM

Dear Colleague,

You are reading this at least one hundred years after the death of the subject of this case history, which occurred in 1909. As I write this in the year after his death, there is no way I can publish this material in a medical journal without violating the privacy of the patient, since in order to convey the unique features of this case, the patient must be identified by his true name. I, instead, am placing the manuscript in trust with the Bank of England to be delivered to the Editor-in-Chief of The Lancet in the year 2009. To him I have transferred the burden of judging whether sufficient time has elapsed to permit making the details of this fascinating case, and the unique treatment my team and I adopted, available to my medical colleagues. I have in past years, when I thought either the pathology involved in a particular case, or the course the treatment took to be of sufficient interest, written up the material in the standard form for a scientific paper and submitted it. This particular case turned out to be so different, both in the patient's pathology and the novel form the treatment took, that I decided to write it in a narrative form. This way I could best convey the evolution of the treatment plan and the excitement it produced in those participating in it.

First, I believe it would be helpful to the reader to know something about me and how I came to be associated with this interesting case.

My name is Brandon Neal. I am a physician, a neurologist. I opened a practice in 1879. Almost from the day I opened my office it was successful – overwhelmingly successful. I am still able to view my good fortune with the honest awareness that I was that rare being, "the right man at the right place at the right time." The "right man" means that I had needs that caused me to be alert to the potential value of a bit of information I chanced upon. The "right place" and the "right time" means that I happened to pass by the bulletin board at St. Thomas Hospital at a time when a notice was posted announcing a series of lectures and demonstrations to be given by Professor Jean Charcot of Salpetriere Hospital in Paris bearing upon his study of the nervous disorder known as hysteria. My small inherited income had permitted me to pack a bag and to head straightaway to Paris.

What I saw and heard at Salpetriere Hospital in those following days affected me profoundly.

Using hypnosis, Charcot was able to eliminate a patient's symptom, be it paralysis of a limb or blindness, demonstrating that the symptom had a psychic rather than a physical etiology. Seeing this happen with my own eyes was a revelation, an epiphany. Inspired, I decided to continue this quest for new knowledge by continuing on to Vienna, Europe's other Mecca of advanced medicine, to see what the famous faculty of its university could add to what I had just learned. While attending a lecture there by Professor Brücke, I was introduced to Brücke's assistant, a man about my own age who had written an elegant scientific paper, which I had chanced to read earlier, on the microscopic anatomy of the nervous system (fishes in this case). I was impressed by the paper's clarity and careful methodology. The young doctor's name was Sigmund Freud.

When Freud learned that I had just come from attending Charcot's lectures, he pressed me to have lunch with him and to describe in detail everything I had seen and heard at Salpetriere. Freud told me that my report clinched the matter for him: He had long wanted to attend Charcot's lectures and was now determined to do so just as soon as he could manage to get a traveling stipend from the university. At this lunch, we discovered a mutual affinity—Freud's perfect English helped—and a regular correspondence was established when I returned to London. I had, in fact, only recently paid Sigmund another visit in Vienna to celebrate the end of his obligatory year of military service. I found that my friend was as excited as ever over the new treatment of hysteria and wanted to know all about my use of it in my new private practice.

Upon returning to London from my first European sojourn, I wrote a scientific paper describing the new ideas and insights I'd gained there. I submitted this paper to the Royal Medical and Chirurgical Society of London, to which I now belonged, and the committee accepted it for reading at the society's next scientific meeting. This was fresh "news from the front." It would be several years before Charcot presented his findings to the French *Academie des sciences*. After that, the whole world would come to know, and a new era in the treatment of mental disorders would begin.

Following my presentation, as often happens, my name became associated with this new therapy from the continent and continental medical discoveries being given more weight at that time than domestic ones, I soon found myself to be the fashionable man to see in London.

Colleagues began to refer patients whom they encountered who manifested hysterical symptoms and soon they made up a large part of my practice. I tried my best to emulate Charcot's technique, but with mixed results. In many instances I could not induce an hypnotic trance. I began to just let them talk and, while to date I have not achieved the relief of hysterical symptoms with this new technique, I discovered that I, and the patients, learned about other areas of conflict in their lives. The patients seemed to benefit from this "ventilating." Word began to spread and people were now coming to me specifically for this "talking treatment." It was at this point in the evolution of my technique that this case history begins.

Brandon Neal, M.D.   London, July 3, 1910

Café Royal, Friday, 4th. February

I was expecting my host of the previous evening to occupy the second chair at my table. I ordered my usual glass of sherry as I waited. I looked around the room and smiled at the sight of a group on the far side of the room—those whom London was referring to as the "aesthetes." I have to admit that the length of my hair approximated theirs. However, I wasn't wearing a mauve jacket as was a voluble and celebrated member of that group. I very purposely wore a conservative grey suit with a muted stripe, the uniform of the professional man. A sad trait but a true one: people tend to believe one's dress reflects one's competence.

The stout well-dressed man in whose home I had witnessed the curious scene the night before entered the Grill Room with an attitude and carriage identifying importance and social substance. He looked about with expectation.

I signaled to him and then motioned to the empty chair at my table. The man, Mr. Mycroft Holmes, with an expression of relief strode across the room, shook my hand and sat down.

In bypassing social niceties, he exposed the level of his anxiety. "Well, Doctor, what can you tell me?"

A waiter came to the table at this very moment and we were forced to turn to the business of ordering our meals. I ordered sole *meuniere* and my guest the jugged hare.

The waiter left and Mycroft Holmes began again. "I know you had very little time to form an opinion last night, but what you did see is pretty typical of his behavior."

I nodded. "Yes, as you say, the opportunity for observation was brief, but curiously complete. It's almost as if your brother made an effort to present a condensed yet accurate picture of his condition. All the salient features were present."

"You don't say."

"Very much so. But before I get into my impression of your brother, you must satisfy my curiosity about that strange phrase he'd written in the book he'd left behind, 'Fishy Fish.'"

The serious demeanor with which Holmes had entered the restaurant was replaced with a short laugh followed by a long sigh and a shaking of his head.

"Several months ago I was forced to take over control of my brother's assets. He had begun to spend great sums on a variety of wild schemes—mostly giving money to sundry people he would only identify as 'agents.' Curiously, he made no protest to my action. It was as if he knew—though couldn't admit—that his behavior was bizarre. Anyway, since that time I have given him a weekly allowance. He insists that it be transmitted in a specific manner. I must put his 'packet' into a book which he has designated the prior week by leaving a note in the book in which he'd received the money the week before. This is what you witnessed last evening. The note is, of course, in code."

Holmes suddenly laughed ruefully, shaking his head again. "Listen to me, I said, 'of course', just as if it's what any normal person would expect."

I fully understood my companion's reaction.

"And, 'fishy fish' is the code for the book into which the money is to be deposited for next week?" I asked.

"Precisely. A clue to the title of the book."

"I understand the process now, but 'fishy fish' still puzzles me."

"I'm not surprised. Sherlock's messages were way above my head until he agreed to limit the books' authors to just three: Thackeray, Trollop and Dickens. Even so I have to spend more time than I can spare trying to figure it out and I must do so, you understand, or he becomes riled."

"Thackeray, Trollop and Dickens," I mused. "Aha! I've got it. 'fishy fish' means Trollop's *Phineus Finn.*"

"Good for you. And you did it without any help. I have a list of all their books written out so that I can run through them each time. Well done, sir."

I began thinking that the case had taken on an entertaining aspect.

"Very well," I said, "You asked me about the impression I gained of your brother last night. Perhaps the best way would be to take you through a review of last evening and point out the meaning a man in my profession puts on the details of your brother's behavior."

"Please do." Mycroft Holmes unbuttoned his coat and sat back in his chair.

"First of all there is the spying on the house disguised as a news vendor. I will come back to the fact that he uses disguises, but for the moment let's consider his spying. You had already told me that your brother, Sherlock . . . that is his name, am I right?"

He nodded.

"Yes, well you had already told me before I came to your home last night that Sherlock seems to be living in a fantasy world in which he is the world's greatest detective. We all, of course, have fantasies about ourselves, imagining our importance to be greater—or less in some cases—than it is in reality."

A frown appeared on the face of Holmes. He was not accustomed to having anyone suggest that he might think more of himself than was true.

"But, you see, your brother is actually acting upon the notion that he is the great detective, and by doing so shows us that for him, mere fantasy has become reality and, therefore, a delusion. In addition, you'll remember he crossed the room and closed the drapes, thus shutting out the enemy in the outside world, enabling him to turn to deal with the one at hand. I'm speaking of myself, of course. Immediately he saw through and rejected the identity you had given me along with the errand you said had brought me to your home. Then he rapidly and in great detail pointed out physical facts he observed about me and proceeded to pronounce his conclusions in no uncertain terms."

Mycroft Holmes shifted in his seat, but remained intently focused on what I was saying.

"Now this to me is very significant," I continued. "Your brother was correct about all of his observations. I had in fact walked to your home and I did cut through a park and I did walk through some mud. I was wearing a pair of Viennese boots and also a Hungarian waistcoat. I'd recently developed photographs, which he deduced, I assume, from the stains the developing solution left on my fingers." I held out my hand and showed my guest a slight yellow discoloration on my right little finger.

"Two things are of great importance here in forming a

diagnosis. The first is his heightened p e r ception, which is typical of someone experiencing mania. Equally significant is his profound certainty about his conclusions—egomania. This moves in the direction of a diagnosis of a serious thinking disorder, a psychosis in fact. In other words, his delusional world has solidly become the real world for him. Your brother has no doubt at all that I am a spy of the Austro-Hungarian Empire, who was sent to London to take pictures of the plans for a new warship and carry them back to my superiors in Vienna.

"He is dead certain about his conclusions—yet he is very wrong. I did not walk through St. James Park as he said, but through Berkeley Square. The path was muddy in one place, but I didn't stop at a duck pond. I bought both my boots and the waistcoat on a recent trip to visit a colleague of mine in Vienna. And I have been dabbling in photography a bit as a hobby, not to photograph plans for warships."

"You mentioned a diagnosis, Doctor. Am I right in thinking you've heard and seen enough to be sure of your opinion?"

The waiter returned with the bottle of claret I'd ordered, sniffed the cork and poured some for me. I motioned for him to go ahead and pour a glass for each of us.

The waiter left and standing now in his place like a genie materialized from out of a bottle, was the tall man who had been sitting with his companions across the room, the one wearing the mauve velvet jacket with the peony in the button hole. His long-cheeked face was broadened in a familiar smile.

"I have come, Brandon, to ask why you have not yet read my book, *Poems*."

"Hello, Oscar. And how do you know I haven't read it already?"

"Because in that case you would have sent 'round a note telling me how brilliant it is."

I laughed. "Yes, you're right, Oscar, I'm sure to have done just that. As it is, I'm still looking forward to that pleasure. I know about it, of course, but haven't yet got a copy."

"An inexcusable negligence, but I suppose one has to make allowances for the busy doctor. I'll see one is sent you."

The man named Oscar shifted his attention to Mycroft Holmes and made a slight inclination of his head. "Mr. Holmes," he said in a perfunctory way and received a frown in return. He returned his gaze again to me, smiled, turned on his heel and left as precipitously as he'd appeared.

"You know Wilde?" asked Mycroft Holmes watching the velvet jacket leave the restaurant.

"An old friend from university days."

"Oxford?"

"No, Trinity. Trinity in Dublin. Our paths parted at the Oxford/Cambridge fork."

"Ah, I see." Mycroft Holmes, who clearly didn't approve of the writer, seemed satisfied that the time of my close acquaintance with Wilde was sufficiently far removed from the present.

"I believe you were about to tell me of the diagnosis you have arrived at, Doctor."

"First, there is more I would like to know about your brother, Mr. Holmes. Tell me something of his past history, the points which seem important to you."

Holmes visibly had to adjust to an unexpected role as historian. He had come to the meeting solely to be the listener. "Well, let me see now, I wasn't prepared for this. Not sure where to begin." His eyes took on a distant focus as he looked into the past. He nodded silently and began, "Of course, the most significant event of his childhood—our childhood—was the death of our mother. I was fourteen. That would make him nine at the time. It was a dreadful blow to both of us, but I think it had a deeper effect . . . a more lasting one on Sherlock.

He seemed to turn inward, while I turned to my friends." Mycroft Holmes paused and took a sip of his wine while he allowed childhood scenes to emerge.

"Our family originates from Yorkshire. After university, my father came to London and became a noted barrister, a QC. Everyone who knew him would agree he was a good man. He tried to be the model of a just and fair professional. He endeavored to avoid a prejudiced treatment of his fellow man—neither unjustly negative nor unjustifiably positive. This also was the form his relationship took with his two sons. We could always rely on his fairness; at the same time we could not expect, nor did we receive, biased fatherly love. Again, I was able to turn elsewhere, but Sherlock wasn't capable of this."

Mycroft saw that I was following every word of his story and this propelled him on.

"I should have come to Sherlock's aid at this point. Perhaps if I had spent more time with him—included him in my circle—but that is water over the dam. He lasted only two years in university, had a horrible experience, didn't make friends there, had unpopular interests—arcane scientific passions and so on. He went to the continent and attended isolated classes taught by controversial and radical professors, mostly in Germany—Heidelberg, Göttingen and the like.

"I lost touch with Sherlock for a number of years. Then four years ago he returned home. Our father had died and I was living in the house bequeathed to both of us. Of course I welcomed him back. Unfortunately, it has not been a scene of brotherly harmony much as I have tried. He is given to periods of deeply low mood and withdraws from everything. During these times he stays in his rooms for weeks, eating little, caring nothing for his appearance or his personal hygiene. He plays his violin for hours on end—Mendelssohn lieder, which play on my nerves—and I fear he is taking some narcotic. Also, and I suppose this is a manifestation of his disorder, he tends to become obsessively involved in one pursuit after another, talking of nothing else. Then he drops that interest and plunges into another as if the first had never existed. At present it is the Mormons of Utah. He has read deeply on the subject and out of it he has evolved a fiction, a story of the tragic abuse of a young girl, complete with named characters. He demands I listen to him. I try to act like I'm paying attention to his ramblings for I'm afraid of offending him, but I have no stomach for it."

I interjected, "Yes, I was going to ask you specifically about the presence of a depressed mood and this further detailed development of a fictional, delusional world is an expected finding."

"Lately," Holmes continued, "he has been talking about moving out of the house so that he can carry out necessary experiments and conduct 'confidential interviews.' He already has his eye on rooms in Baker Street. I'm afraid of a worsening of his condition in a setting that I am unable to monitor. As it is, he has been doing things that could cause me social harm— something I can ill afford—going about in disguises around ministry offices and such. No amount of effort on my part dissuades him one particle from this behavior. Luckily my college roommate and close friend is now the Home Secretary, who has intervened on Sherlock's behalf with Scotland Yard. Two inspectors, Lestrade and Gregson, have been assigned to be the officers to respond when Sherlock has perpetrated some new incident. How long this special treatment can be expected is questionable Without it . . . I don't like to think. Dr. Neal, I'm very worried."

"Indeed you well might be," I sympathized.

I hesitated to tell this likeable man what I really thought. I would have to tell him that the wide mood swings accompanied by the paranoid thinking that he had described were the symptoms of a serious mental disorder, a psychosis (to use the new word for insanity) for which there was no currently effective treatment, a condition which would in the end render the sufferer a creature barely recognizable as human.

At any rate, Sherlock Holmes was not a candidate for the kind of treatment I was using, and also not suitable for Charcot's hypnosis. Charcot had warned of the disastrous consequences of placing a person bordering on a psychosis under hypnosis.

"Yes, your concern is warranted, and I strongly advise that your brother is in need of a rest in a supportive setting. I know of an excellent place in Switzerland. I am willing to . . ."

"No. Don't say it. I could never put Sherlock in a lunatic asylum. It's unthinkable."

I understood. The existing asylums were little more than human warehouses, patients left to the caprices of attendants for the most part.

"The hospital I have in mind is not at all the hellish kind of place you've heard about."

"Nevertheless, I can't countenance such an action, but I know something must be done. The situation is growing worse, entirely unpredictable and bizarre. I have to go each day to my duties at the Ministry with growing concern about what he is up to."

"You may reconsider when I tell you of an additional impression I have. You see, Mr. Holmes, I see signs that his condition may be entering into a pernicious phase. You'll remember I said I would have more to say about the element of the disguises that your brother assumes. I believe his use of disguises represents the beginning of a splitting of his personality. A paranoid psychosis begins when a person's mind fatigues, as it were, in its effort to come to terms with a particularly repugnant feeling or thought that he or she harbors. The paranoid solution is to believe that the repugnant thought is not inside *me*, but out there in the outside world. Outside me is the evil. Outside me is the enemy. Do you follow me, Mr. Holmes?"

"Yes, I think so."

"This process begins with fairly well circumscribed 'enemies:' a neighbor, a political figure, a religious group. But the internal wall thus built around the feared feeling or idea may weaken and threaten to disintegrate altogether. At this point the fragile mind broadens the scope of the imagined persecution and an ominous retreat from reality begins. I believe you can see what this leads to."

"Yes, you are saying the whole world may have to be included in the delusion."

"Exactly. Once this happens, that person is lost to us, never to be part of our world again."

"You think that Sherlock is moving in that direction?"

"That is my fear. This brings another concern to mind. It is clear that I have been included in the group of 'enemies.' Last night I came into your home and you gave me a bogus identity. A terrible strain must have been put on your brother's hold on reality by requiring it to keep you free from taint—a need which must be very strong indeed—while at the same time accounting for your relationship with me. It is imperative that you not become an 'enemy.' I believe, therefore, that we must never be seen together again. That is why I advised you to take such elaborate precautions against being followed when you came here today. I also took care that I was not followed when I left your home last evening. As I just explained, strain on your relationship with your brother has already been engendered by your introducing me as your acquaintance. This must be undone if possible. Therefore I believe you must arrange for an official appearing document from your Ministry's security division, which informs you that Mr. George Andrews has been unmasked as an agent of the Austro-Hungarian Empire, that he narrowly escaped arrest and managed to slip out of the country and back to Austria. You, of course, will act outraged when you show your brother the document. Of course, this will require convincing acting on your part."

Mycroft Holmes was a man of action, one who out of necessity had become a crafty political animal very familiar with the need for secrecy and, at times, less than truthful public statements. He nodded his understanding, yet he was clearly shaken by what he had just been told.

I realized just how overwhelming this information must have been. So, I assumed a more familiar and sympathetic tone.

"Taking the steps to place a brother into a hospital against his will is a most difficult decision. In my experience, once in a protective setting, the patient experiences relief and becomes better able to achieve stability. I hope, after hearing my concerns, you can now understand how important it is to reduce the strain placed upon your brother in every way you can. A good hospital can be a refuge for him."

His lips pressed together like a child refusing cod liver oil. I detected something in his reluctance that told me it was not only his brother about whom he was concerned. Mycroft Holmes was also worried about how it would appear to his associates if he had a brother who had to be confined in an insane asylum. After all, the reigning medical opinion was that mental illness represented the emergence of a degenerate familial trait.

"As I said, I know of such a place in Switzerland, Bellevue Sanitarium . . ."

"Even so. I came to you, Dr. Neal, because I was told of your expertise in a new type of treatment. By using hypnosis you discover the cause of a mental disorder and remove it, thus opening the path back to health. Why can't my brother profit from this treatment?"

I now clearly understood that he would hear any insistence on my part of the inadvisability of such an undertaking as evidence of either a rejection of him and his brother or of my incompetence, neither being a good impression with which to leave someone with such importance and influence as Mr. Mycroft Holmes.

Fortunately the meal came and was served, interrupting our discussion and providing enough of a break to enable me to have the time to consider an alternative to offer Holmes. I waited to speak until the waiter replenished our wine glasses and left.

"It is my view that your brother, Sherlock, is in need of a period of rest at this time. I'm afraid that the kind of therapy I do would not be helpful to him, but I have a Viennese colleague—the one I mentioned earlier—who knows the new treatment and its limitations very thoroughly. I can consult with him. I will write him today with a full description of your brother's clinical picture and I'll ask for his recommendation."

Holmes brightened immediately.

I knew that Sigmund hadn't the experience with hypnosis that I alleged, but I did believe Sigmund knew enough already to know that hypnosis should not be attempted with a pre-psychotic patient. Charcot was obviously the one to consult, but although I knew French well enough to understand a lecture, I shied away from sending the great man an incompetently written letter.

"Thank you, Doctor. I'm sure you realize that I am in a position to use our diplomatic pouch. It is the fastest method to get a letter to Vienna."

The ball had been quickly returned to my court so I felt I must respond in kind. "I will have the letter at your office this afternoon."

With some relief, we each ate our meal, Mycroft Holmes in the hope that he might yet find a solution to help his brother without causing embarrassment to himself, and I, because I had found a way to shift the onus of being the one to pronounce a dreaded diagnosis and a hopeless prognosis away from myself and onto the corroboration of a colleague, and from there onto the limitations of medical science and finally to life's unfairness.

Monday, 7th. February

In the afternoon post, I received a letter at my Harley Street office from a Dr. John Watson. My office assistant handed it to me as I came out of my consulting room between appointments with patients. I didn't recognize the name and curious, I opened it while standing at her desk. The letter's author explained that he had recently arrived in London from India where he had served for a short time as an army medical officer. The letter went on to say that as a result of a bullet wound suffered at the battle of Maiwand in Afghanistan, followed by a near fatal fever, he had been sent to the military hospital at Peshawar. There he'd come under the care of my stepfather, Dr. Albert Morris. During the several months of his convalescence, he and Dr. Morris had become friends. When he left the hospital to return on indefinite medical leave to England, Dr. Morris asked him to visit me, his stepson, and deliver a present to me. Dr. Watson's letter concluded by stating it was also his wish to meet me, about whom my stepfather had spoken so warmly.

I was excited at the prospect of learning first-hand news about my stepfather and straightaway wrote a note inviting Dr. Watson to join me for lunch at the Café Royal the next day and asked my assistant to post it immediately.

Café Royal, Tuesday, 8th. February

The man who was shown to my table still showed the signs of the ravages of injury and serious infection. He must have been no more than thirty and at one time had certainly carried himself with a military bearing, yet was now reduced to a frail man who moved as if middle-aged. His bright blue eyes carried a straight-forward honesty. His ready smile and manner led me to the snap judgment that Dr. Watson was an unaffected man of simple tastes and solid common sense.

We talked easily for a while about India, Dr. Watson's adventures and of his admiration for my stepfather. After a socially appropriate period of conversation for a first meeting with a stranger, Dr. Watson unwrapped the parcel he had brought with him. He laid a wooden box the size of a hymnal on the table.

It was made of a dark wood, possibly teak, and bound in brass. By moving a small brass turtle's body to one side, I found that I was able to open the catch on the lid revealing a black lacquer interior.

"What a delightful box," I declared.

"Albert thought it would come in handy for links, shirt buttons, that sort of thing."

"I will write to him tonight and thank him, and I thank you for carrying it half-way around the globe."

"My pleasure entirely."

I had a high regard for my stepfather, but we had never had the opportunity to become very close. When I was nineteen and already away from home at college, Morris, a physician practicing in London, had married my mother, a widow of five years. Tragically, it was only three years later that she died in a fall from a horse. Albert Morris was hit hard by his loss, causing him to lose interest in other areas of his life including his medical practice. A friend recommended a complete change of pace and scene. Morris decided that his friend was right and India and the military seemed made to order. That had been nine years ago.

"What are your plans now, Dr. Watson?"

"There you've hit the matter squarely. I find that I have been unable to answer that question for myself yet. I have not sufficiently recovered my health to feel the energy or interest to return to active duty or if I were to leave the service permanently, to return to a medical practice. I have no friends here in the city any longer. I trained here, but I left immediately afterward for India. The few people with whom I kept in touch now live elsewhere."

I recognized a note of desperation in the flow of concerns that my question had tapped.

The doctor continued, "I grew up in a small town in the Midlands and can't see myself in that setting again. London is stimulating, but it is expensive—at least staying at a hotel as I have been since arriving back. My pension from the service could provide for an adequate life—if coupled with thrift—and if I could find a compatible person with whom to share lodgings."

I had sympathy for the other man's dilemma and knew the facts he had just recited were ones he had reviewed frequently without resolution. I imagined myself lonely and marginally making ends meet in an impersonal swarm of Londoners. It became clear to me that the gift my stepfather sent was really a method devised to be sure Watson would contact me. Albert Morris wanted to provide his ailing friend with at least one person in the city who would know his name.

For a while we both concentrated on the food the

waiter had brought. I began wondering how I could help this agreeable man. I was not about to become the room-mate Dr. Watson sought. I was happy in my bachelor diggings.

"I can't think of anyone looking for a shared living arrangement, but I will certainly keep my ears open. I hope, however, that you like the theater—plays and opera—for I have a good friend who has a share in a ticket agency, who offers me unsold tickets gratis on a regular basis. It would give me much pleasure if you would go with me when you're not busy."

Obvious pleasure in his voice, John Watson declared, "It has been a long time since I've seen any entertainment save the usual round of songs at the officers' club. I frequently attended plays and the opera whenever I could as a student at St. Bart's —standing room, of course."

"Then it's settled. I have your address and as soon as my friend next has some tickets I'll send a message. Frequently it's on short notice and many times they're not the best seats, you understand."

"Of course, of course, I understand. Capital!"

The rest of the meal was spent in small talk. I decided I had found a very amicable gentleman with whom to pass an evening. I, of course, had no friend who had free tickets to give away, but believed that John Watson, who certainly couldn't afford the theater himself, would be uncomfortable if he knew I was buying them. A white lie, but one that just might lift his spirits until he was able to make some friends of his own.

Friday, 11th. February

At mid-morning my office assistant knocked on my consulting room door and I called out, "Yes?"

She opened the door, stepped inside, closed it again. "There is a messenger here from a Mr. Mycroft Holmes."

"Really? So soon! Ask him to come in."

A young man entered and handed me a sealed envelope. I broke the seal and read the enclosed letter.

"My dear Dr. Neal,

A reply to your letter to Vienna has come in the diplomatic pouch this morning. Please tell my messenger—who was carefully instructed to avoid being followed—when I may expect you at my office today. In order to keep our meeting unknown to my brother, you should enter the building lying just east of the Ministry through its back entrance. Ask the doorman for the Special Maintenance Office.

M. Holmes."

I was put off by the man's presumption that I should be at his beck-and-call, but I counseled myself that the elder Holmes was very anxious for a solution to his problem, and I also reminded myself that he was a man accustomed to having others snap-to whenever he wanted anything done. I had an appointment at the hospital at four. I told the messenger to report to Mr. Holmes I'd meet him at one-fifteen.

At a quarter to one, I came out of my building and hailed a hansom to take me to Whitehall and the Ministry. Every type of vehicle crowded the street making the going slow. The cabbie worked constantly, urging the horse forward into any small opening in the traffic. I drifted into an oblivion of the tumult around me and into speculation about the reply I had received from my Viennese friend, Sigmund. My judgment, as I've said, was that Sherlock Holmes would be an impossible patient for hypnosis. I would never dare to put him in a hypnotic trance. Whatever hold the man had on reality might be dissolved in an instant. In addition, Holmes's obvious narcissism and nascent paranoia would make the necessary therapeutic relationship required for my new "talking therapy" impossible. I hoped Sigmund wouldn't, out of enthusiasm for the new ideas, recommend hypnosis for Sherlock Holmes.

The day was blustery, making me grab for my hat when I alighted from the cab at the back entrance to the building I'd been instructed to enter. The doorman watched my buffeted ascent of the steps with amusement, opening the door for me at the last moment.

I asked him to direct me to the Special Maintenance Office. My mention of this, to my mind humble destination, caused a different reaction in the doorman, whose attitude visibly changed to one of respect. I was directed to the basement where I found the door marked "Maintenance" to be locked. I stood in the hallway for several minutes before I heard my name called out in a loud whisper. I looked around and saw Mycroft Holmes peering from a partially opened door farther along the deserted hallway. A sign on the door read "Storage." Holmes held the door open to admit me and then closed it and checked to be sure it was locked. Satisfied, he turned to me and held out his hand.

"Please excuse the unusual welcome, but you did stress that we must keep Sherlock in the dark about our meetings. This is the entrance to a tunnel between this building and the Ministry." He held out two keys. "Few of us have access. I'm giving you two keys, which I'll need back later. The brass key is to this door. The other key is to a door we'll come to in a moment that opens onto a stairway, which ascends to an alcove immediately behind my office. I'm certain Sherlock knows nothing of the tunnel or the stairs."

I took the keys and followed Mycroft Holmes along the dimly-lit passage. After thirty yards or so, closed doors began to appear along the tunnel's course.

"Fourth on the right, got that?" asked Mycroft. "Try your key."

I did so and the lock tumblers turned easily.

"Right. Now a three-story climb," said Holmes.

He led the way, gaslights at long intervals lighting the steep stairway. At the top, we stepped into a small room no wider than a hallway. Two straight-back chairs had been placed tight to one wall. Across from them was a door.

Mycroft paused to catch his breath after the climb. "When you're here, just pull this cord. It rings a small bell in my office."

We both passed through into Mycroft's large office. It was furnished much like the drawing room in his home. A large Persian carpet that could easily have come from a sultan's palace covered the floor. A coal fire burned cheerfully in the fireplace. Looking back at the door Mycroft had just closed, I saw that on the office side it was made to look like part of a bookcase.

"Yes, Doctor, it's a secret passage, just like in novels. Please have a seat," he said as he advanced to his desk. Over his shoulder he added, "There's whisky in the decanter. Please help yourself."

"Not at the moment, thank you." I picked out a small leather armchair and sat down.

Mycroft unlocked a drawer in his desk and took out a large liver-colored envelope. He came around the desk holding it in one hand with a cigar humidor in the other, which he extended toward me, but I declined. Holmes handed over the envelope and commenced lighting his cigar. I broke the pasted paper seal and withdrew another sealed envelope. I recognized the handwriting, now familiar to me through our regular correspondence.

Mycroft sat in a chair opposite me and watched while creating a grand cloud of cigar smoke. Within the envelope was a single sheet. As were all the letters from Sigmund, it was in English. My impulse was to read the letter first to myself, so anxious was I to discover Sigmund's opinion, but sensing that Holmes regarded the letter to be addressed to him as well, I read it aloud.

"My dear Brandon,

I gathered by the urgency of your letter and the manner of its delivery that you want an immediate

and direct clinical impression from me regarding the case material you presented in your usual pithy style. I hope you don't mind that I conferred with Professor Meynert, the Chairman of the Psychiatry Department. He concurs entirely with my view that the gentleman you describe is suffering the early stage of a cyclical disorder, mania alternating with melancholia. The grandiosity and suspicious trend—paranoia to use the new term—is an ominous sign. Both Meynert and I emphatically recommend that any procedure such as hypnosis, which weakens the patient's tenuous hold over his mind and hence on reality, not be attempted. Such a course of therapy would surely hasten the deepening of the illness. In any case it is not possible, because the feelings he would develop toward his doctor would quickly be invaded by his paranoia and he would flee treatment. The therapist would quickly be included in a pernicious, delusional system. This man can most be helped by finding a way, if possible, to wall off the paranoia at its present level. Many sufferers of this disorder do this on their own, as you very well know, by joining cults, or through religious fanaticism. Hopefully you can think of an appropriate vehicle for this man, whom I gather from your description to be of high intelligence and culture. You are in an enviable position to study this as yet poorly understood disorder.

I send my heartfelt regards and warmly await your next visit to Vienna. Your friend,

Sigmund"

I looked up to see a crestfallen man in the opposite chair.

"Then, it's as you said," Holmes mumbled in despair. "I really am at my wit's end. Night before last I entertained the ambassadors of two key European nations at my home. I discovered, upon seeing them ushered into the drawing room, that it was by Sherlock appropriately attired as the butler. Naturally I said nothing, but it quite unnerved me. I was not afterward at my best trying to negotiate some very delicate matters for her Majesty's government. And then, yesterday afternoon, I spotted him here in the building, disguised as a porter."

Mycroft looked sharply toward me, adding, "Don't worry. As I told you, two inspectors have been assigned to cooperate with me. Knowing you were coming here, I took the precaution of asking Inspector Lestrade to make an appointment to call on Sherlock at home at two p.m. today to consult with him on the subject of tropical poisons. I didn't tell you, but my brother considers himself the leading expert on such subjects as tropical poisons and such trivia as cigar ash.

"But of more heightened concern to me is the matter I mentioned to you already, that of his decision to move out of our house. He has placed an advertisement in the paper seeking a roommate. Fortunately, the requirements he cites are such that he hasn't yet had an answer."

"What requirements does he list?"

Mycroft laughed out loud in spite of his depressed spirits.

"He states that the fellow must be of good character, must tolerate strong, navy-cut tobacco, be willing to absent himself from the premises whenever Sherlock interviews clients, have no objection to violin playing at any hour of the day or night and finally have no problem with Sherlock conducting chemical experiments in their rooms, experiments producing noxious fumes."

I couldn't help laughing out loud also. "I don't think you need worry about his moving out soon."

Deeply aware of the seriousness of the situation that had been presented to me, I quickly became sober. "I think my colleague's suggestion about walling off—

isolating—your brother's paranoid system is what we must concentrate on. I developed a vague notion along this line in the days after we met for lunch, but just now it came to me what form that concentration should naturally take. The evil which your brother is trying to project outward away from himself has taken on the persona of the criminal. His desperately desired mastery over this 'evil self' has led to the invention of his imagined identity as 'the world's greatest detective.'"

My presentation of this insight had followed closely upon its very formation in my mind. I believe my excitement over this synthesis must have been evident in my voice.

"Don't you see, we must reinforce his delusion so that it remains in a circumscribed and therefore, manageable form?"

"No I don't see," answered my troubled listener. "You seem to be saying that we must make him more deranged."

"In a way, that is so, but by deepening the faith in his own delusional solution, we cause his psyche to have confidence that this narrowly defined delusion is strong enough as it is and need not undergo further extension into broader aspects of his life."

I discerned that Holmes was struggling to

understand. What was familiar to me must sound like arcane gibberish to him.

"What I'm talking about is what parents intuitively do all the time with children when they reinforce the child's confidence by fostering an exaggerated belief. 'Oh, what a wonderful runner you are.' Such a timely, intuitive remark might at that moment prevent a regression in the child's self-confidence that in turn would lead to a less adaptive behavior such as crying and clinging to the mother."

Mycroft Holmes sat silently studying my face while rolling his cigar between thumb and fingers, and then he slowly began to nod. "Yes, I think I see what you mean. When I first went to Harrow, I was so frightened and unhappy I thought I would have to run away. Then the rugby captain came to me and said that, because of my size and strength, the school would come to depend on me in the following years. This faith I thought he had in me, which I now recognize could have been no more than an off-hand comment to a hulking new-boy, caused me to feel a new worth and I settled right down. I had confidence that I was a valued member of the group. It's something like this that you're talking about, isn't it?"

"Very much like that. And, just suppose that it had been the headmaster who'd become aware of your personal crisis and had told the rugger captain to go to you with those words. That would parallel the manipulation I am suggesting we set out to do. In fact, probably intuitively, you have already made a good beginning in having Inspector Lestrade call on your brother for consultation, strengthening your brother's idea that he is valued by the police." Then a further thought struck me. "Ah ha! He already believes himself to be the world's greatest detective. We will give him the additional identity of the world's first 'consulting detective.'"

"By Jove! I've got the hang of it," said Mycroft Holmes. "Is there something else we should be doing now?"

"We will have to be careful to proceed slowly, for your brother is a brilliant man and an uncanny observer of details. It would be very easy to blunder and give the game away. If that happened, his paranoia would catch fire like dry kindling. We are really about to embark upon a delicate operation, the failure of which could mean your brother's very life."

Mycroft's rising hope tumbled and with it his returning anxiety showed on his face.

"But we don't intend to blunder," I said with enthusiasm. "And, I just had a thought which might solve one of the immediate problems. Several days ago I lunched with an army medical officer recently returned from India where he was confined for some time to a military hospital. My stepfather was his physician. The occasion of our meeting was his delivery to me of a gift from my stepfather. The serendipitous part of this story is that the man, Dr. John Watson, is looking for a gentleman with whom to share lodgings as he is trying to maintain himself on his army pension. I guess it was when you were listing your brother's published requirements for a roommate that the idea formed in my mind that only a 'keeper' would agree to Sherlock's terms. I have no idea, of course, if Dr. Watson would consider the role of monitor and companion to a patient with what are sure to be very trying behaviors, but if he did . . . well, what could better serve our purpose?"

A proposition had been presented to Mycroft and this brought forth the wariness of a man who has had to make hundreds of high-level decisions. "Tell me more about this Dr. Watson."

"I don't know much about him really, only an impression. The fact I do know, and to my mind it counts for much, is that my stepfather sent him to me. He was with Watson for months while he was hospitalized and would have had the chance to get to know him well. If he had any doubts about the man he never would have put us in touch. Now then, as to my actual observation of him: He seemed a reserved man of simple tastes, open and honest, bright but not intellectual, of sound common sense. I thought him to be no man's fool, but ready to give a stranger the benefit of the doubt."

"My God man!" cried Mycroft Holmes, "You've just described the ideal Briton. He should have his likeness struck onto the gold sovereign." He struck his knee with his open hand. "By all means sound out Dr. Watson and see if he will sign up for his next posting."

"I believe he will be inclined to take it on. My impression is that he strongly identifies himself with the medical fraternity and would like to return to practice were it not for the debilitation of his recent illness. I will present our proposition in a way which will play to that wish."

"Also, Dr. Neal, there is this," said Holmes. "You say he is trying to get by on his army pension. That could be little more than genteel survival. What I will be asking him to do amounts to a professional undertaking and I will pay him liberally."

I considered this. "The matter of payment must be handled very tactfully, I feel. He might be offended if he thought any charity was intended. We might, however, make clear that the apartment would be a place you were leasing for the purpose of your brother's monitored care. Dr. Watson should easily agree to your paying the full rent with an additional stipend for his board."

"Yes, I see your point. That is certainly the minimum. Understand, I don't consider that to be adequate recompense for the doctor's round-the-clock supervision, but it's a place to start, and one that should not arouse objection. Yes, yes, my dear sir, please lose no time in launching our plan."

Saturday, 12th. February

At Watson's suggestion, the meeting I requested for the next evening was held at a small tearoom in Goodge Street near Watson's hotel. It was chosen for its convenience, but it also fit Watson's purse.

I decided to walk the several blocks to the meeting place. The mild evening was a pleasant surprise to Londoners after the inclement weather of the previous day. On the walk from my apartment in Upper Wimpole Street I had been musing about how I had arrived at my present involvement in the case of Mr. Sherlock Holmes. It was with some chagrin that I admitted to myself that my involvement had taken its present form, because I hadn't wanted to complicate my comfortable medical practice—my tidy, lucrative medical practice—by taking on the attempted treatment of a patient as seriously ill as the younger Holmes. There is something about passing from a condition of possessing but a thin purse to that of enjoying a fat one that creates momentum in that direction, a momentum with which one is loath to tamper. My impulse to write to Sigmund was in order to gain support for my backing out of any ill-advised attempt to treat a case of incipient psychosis with my method of therapy.

An accident at the corner of Cavendish and Langham Place interrupted my reflections. A Whitbread's Brewery wagon had collided with an omnibus. The only casualties were four casks of Whitbread's Best Bitter, which had rolled off the rear of the wagon and broken apart on the pavement. For a minute, I became one of a crowd of helpless men who watched mournfully as the gallons of fragrant beer washed by us in the gutter.

"Quick, fetch me a mug!" the man standing next to me shouted.

Smiling, I resumed my walk, musing about Sherlock Holmes and Sigmund's reply. Yes, I believed it was his reply that reminded me that my Austrian friend and I were in on the exciting, embryonic phase of a new science of the mind. No longer were mental disorders to be ascribed to exterior agents—phases of the moon, possession of demons and curses—or be ascribed to the patient's inherent mental inferiority. Now the investigator looked inward to the patient's own experiences and reactions for the source of the problem. As I read Freud's letter I saw that I was indeed in a privileged position to observe and contribute to the knowledge about both the cause and treatment of a major mental disorder. I began to feel a *call* to undertake the challenge.

With a quickened step and new enthusiasm I traversed the length of Mortimer Street and found the narrow façade of the Milton Tearoom at the beginning of Goodge Street. A tall lace-curtained window told me what to expect inside.

I had exchanged my business suit for a soft shooting jacket. Watson wore the same suit he had worn at our first meeting, the only civilian clothes he owned no doubt.

After we had been served a pot of tea and Watson, acting as "mother," was pouring some for each of us, I said in a voice that conveyed a change of direction, "I'm obliged to admit to you my friend, that I come here this evening flying false colors."

Watson looked up, surprised.

"While I am very pleased to be able to sit down with you for some conversation, I have, in fact, come to see if you will agree to help me with a medical problem— a case I've been brought in on."

Instant interest appeared on John Watson's face, undoubtedly more than had shown there in many months. "Medical problem, you say?"

"Yes, but you understand that what I'm about to tell you must be treated as a privileged communication."

"Just so!"

I proceeded to tell him all I knew about the case of Sherlock Holmes. Included was the idea I proposed to Mycroft of asking Watson if he would consider taking on the role of live-in physician/monitor. I mentioned that as a matter of course Mycroft Holmes would be paying the full rent for the apartment. I omitted the full discussion I'd had with Mycroft about remuneration.

"Fascinating!" Watson murmured when I finished my tale. After sitting in silent contemplation for a few moments, he chuckled and added, "Must have been an anxious moment, reading that letter aloud to Mr. Holmes before you knew that your Viennese friend agreed with you."

I laughed. "You have that right."

"As I understand it, you want me to be there to observe him and in some way to cause him to concentrate his delusional illness into his very own idea of being the great detective. What I'm not clear about is how I'm to go about promoting this, ah, 'concentrating.'"

"Nor am I, at least not yet. I have never attempted anything of the kind before and here I need your help. The treatment plan, as it were, is just in the process of being drawn up between us as we sit here. I have only had fragmentary ideas. Walking over here I was turning over in my mind something Mycroft Holmes told me. He had arranged to have a Scotland Yard detective consult Sherlock on the subject of tropical poisons, a knowledge of which he prides himself. Intuitively, I think, Mycroft had hit upon a way of supporting the delusion. You agree with me that the paranoid system will spread if it is failing to hold its ground, so to speak, just as an army must fall back once it sees its defenses breached?"

Dr. Watson nodded his understanding. "Right. As you were speaking, Arthur Potter came to mind. When I was a boy, Arthur was our town's madman. Now, of course, I would diagnose his condition as chronic *dementia praecox*. But what I was reminded of just now is that for the time I knew him, his condition remained stable, and while I never really thought of it before, I believe this may have been because the people of the town all supported his delusional system. Arthur thought he ran the British government. Each day he sent a 'dispatch' to the Prime Minister or the Queen. The post-mistress, who ran the postal office out of a corner of her yarn and dry goods shop, would accept the letters and, I imagine after having a good laugh, destroy them. His letters were easy to identify; they bore no stamp and the return address was simply, 'Arthur.' When folks encountered Arthur they seriously inquired about the state of affairs in the country. I heard my Dad say to Arthur once that he rested easier at night knowing he, Arthur, was looking after all of us. I never witnessed anyone laugh at him, not even one of us lads. The town never challenged Arthur's self-importance.

"Your description of Sherlock Holmes has him running all over the place with little organization—a little spying here, a little disguise work there—quite higgledy-piggledy." A look of excitement bloomed on John Watson's face. "What the chap needs is a real case to concentrate on."

Excitement spread to me. "Exactly! That's what Sherlock Holmes needs. He needs a real case!"

"John . . . I hope you don't mind my calling you,

John."

"I'd be most happy if you would, Brandon."

"John, I think you've hit upon the vital ingredient in the treatment. I have no idea at all how this can be done, but we must find a way."

I had become aware that John Watson was no longer just a passive participant; in him I had discovered a true partner.

"I want to be sure that I understand you correctly. You are, then, agreeing to share rooms with our patient and take upon yourself the role of observing him and forwarding our treatment plan—as much as our planned manipulation of his environment can be called treatment. I hope this is true."

"It is indeed, and, I might add, I'm very pleased that you want me on the team. I suppose my first act is to answer Holmes's advertisement."

"Yes, and it should be today before someone with an unbelievable tolerance for narcissism, foul tobacco, violin scraping and poisonous chemical fumes opts to share the lodging."

I discerned a newfound energy evident in Watson's person. Bright interest showed in his eyes.

"May I ask what you are thinking, John?"

He chuckled, "My dear fellow, I was only

anticipating the coming interview."

Monday, 14th. February

After our meeting Saturday evening, Watson answered Sherlock's advertisement, stating he was an army surgeon on indefinite but probably permanent medical leave from the service, who was seeking to share lodgings. He emphasized that he was not an invalid and was completely up to any physical tasks that might be required by the living arrangement. He received a rapid response by messenger asking him to meet Holmes today in one of the laboratories at St. Bartholomew's Hospital. The following is his report to me of that occasion.

Many times it is an insignificant feature of a person or place that comes to form its most powerful essence for us: a slight mannerism, the sound of a step, the smell of a season. Watson said he experienced this when he passed through the gateway into St. Barts to keep his morning appointment with Holmes. How many times had he passed that way in his years of training?

Standing beneath the arch, John heard his name

called out and turned to see Stamford, his wound dresser during his last year at St. Bart's. After the "How have you been?" questions had been covered, Stamford asked why Watson was visiting the hospital and Watson told him of his appointment with Sherlock Holmes and the reason.

Stamford then said, "I should warn you, John, Holmes is only ten to the dozen, not someone I would want to share rooms with,"

"Really? Why do you say that?"

"He has some very strange ideas. He goes on maniacally about odd branches of science. On the other hand, he seems honest enough."

"Let me see if I can summarize your opinion of Sherlock Holmes—an honest maniac. That about it?"

Stamford had laughed. "Not quite. A cold-blooded, honest maniac."

"Cold-blooded?"

"I mean in his aloofness about the propriety of his scientific interests. It's well and good to be unemotional and unbiased in one's scientific investigation, but Holmes takes it a bit far if you ask me. For instance, I saw him in the morgue with my own eyes beating cadavers with a stick in order to ascertain the degree of bruising that is possible after death."

Stamford then added, "You see, I can imagine him giving a friend a near lethal dose of an alkaloid, just to be able to observe the reaction. Not out of malice, you understand, but only out of unbridled curiosity."

"Good grief! A medical student, I suppose."

"No. Heaven only knows what the object of his studies is. But here we are. You must form your own opinion about him, but remember, you have been warned."

Stamford led the way into the building and down a whitewashed corridor that was familiar ground to Watson. At the further end, a low arched passage led to the chemical laboratory, a lofty chamber lined and littered with countless bottles. Broad, low tables were scattered about, which bristled with retorts, test tubes and Bunsen lamps, their blue flames flickering. There was only one man in the room. He was bent over a distant table absorbed in his work. At the sound of their steps he glanced around and sprang to his feet with a cry of excited pleasure.

"I've found it! I've found it! I have found a reagent which is precipitated by hemoglobin and by nothing else."

Had he discovered a gold mine, Watson thought, greater delight could not have shown upon his face.

Stamford then made the introduction, "Dr.

Watson, Mr. Sherlock Holmes."

"How are you? You have been to Afghanistan, I perceive."

"Why, yes, but how on earth did you know?" Watson gasped, truly surprised and puzzled.

"Never mind," replied the man he had come to meet. "If you'll excuse me a moment, I have to attend to the final stages of my experiment on hemoglobin."

Stamford smiled meaningfully and said, "I must be going, old chap. Nice to see you again, John," and left.

Holmes, holding up a test tube, strode back over to where Watson waited. "Now, at last, there is a test for human blood. No longer must a detective gaze helplessly at crime-scene blood, not knowing if it comes from the victim or a chicken." With this, he dropped a few white crystals into the test tube followed by a few drops of a clear fluid and immediately the solution turned a mahogany color. "There, you see, and it's sensitive to one part in a million."

"Remarkable!"

Holmes lowered the test tube. "And now the apartment." He placed the test tube in a rack on the laboratory bench, turned off the Bunsen burner under an Erlenmeyer flask, removed his apron and in an instant donned his jacket. "Shall we go? 221B Baker Street. I'm sure you'll find the rooms very comfortable."

Off balance, John could only stammer, 'Yes, yes, of course."

This report of his first meeting with Sherlock Holmes was given me by an elated John Watson later that same day at the Milton Tearoom.

He had broken off his story to pour both of us tea. He stirred milk and sugar into his cup and then sat back, thinking a bit before going on.

"A dizzying experience. I do hope I'm up to the assignment. It's a good thing I had been open with him about my background, because he divined, by some amazing means, more about me than I knew myself. He even knew the year I finished my medical degree at the University of London, 1878. And, I might add, he is most pleased when he sees that he has amazed me. Of course, he appears to brush aside any astonishment of mine.

"But, the main thing is that he seems genuinely pleased with the living arrangement. I believe I am successfully installed in my new role."

"You went with him to the rooms he's interested in taking in Baker Street?"

"That I did, and a comfortable set of rooms they are and the landlady, Mrs. Hudson, seems to be someone who is both friendly yet respects a man's privacy. On the other hand, Sherlock Holmes is a curious piece of work. He clearly thinks he stands above the rest of us mortals, but then he does something quite unexpected like giving me the pick of the two bedrooms. And then in the next moment, in no uncertain terms, he tells me he *will* use the sitting-room table to conduct his chemical experiments.

"Perhaps you'll think this sentimentally premature but, in spite of his overarching egoism, I like the man I see behind the illness. I have no doubt that I will be able to bear with his trying behavior."

"Excellent. We couldn't ask for a better beginning. Now let me tell you about the meeting I had today with Mycroft Holmes—in his office once again. This is my day off, so I could devote the whole day to our project."

Now that Watson was a committed participant in the enterprise and knowing he would enjoy the description, I told him of the secret tunnel and stairway to Mycroft's office at the Ministry. Watson punctuated the tale with an astonished, "Upon my word," and, "You don't say!"

"I'm happy to be able to report that your suggestion to find a real case for our patient advanced nicely. First, I delicately asked Mycroft just how much influence he had with the police. He asked what I had in mind and I told him about our strategy.

"'You'll have no problem with the police,'" he told me. "'Inspectors Lestrade and Gregson are good men, but like all men they are interested in their own advancement. To some degree, they will resent having to add the demands of amateurs to their own required official duties, but at the same time they know they are putting their highest boss, the Home Secretary, in their debt.

'The Home Secretary," Mycroft said to me with a wink, "is already very deeply in mine for past favors, so we have a vast reservoir to draw upon.'"

John's face reflected the pleasure he must have felt in having such influential teammates.

"Wanting to put our plan into action as soon as possible," I said, "I arranged to meet Lestrade and Gregson together later in the afternoon. I'm sure you can picture the scene. Proposing to them that they participate in our scheme was like asking bare-knuckle boxers to take ballet lessons. They were very uncomfortable sitting there listening to me. I explained my diagnosis and our plan to provide Sherlock with a 'real' case. I'm sure they thought it was I who was the patient. But I came up with an analogy, which happily did the trick. I asked them to imagine they had an old grandfather living at their home, a man who was depressed because he felt himself to be worthless. You suggest to him that he grow flowers in the back garden and sell them in order to make a contribution to the household income. He is pleased with the idea of becoming of value to the family. The problem is the flowers will now have to be sold so he'll see that his contribution is real—that you have not lied to him about his value to the family. What would you gentlemen do?" I asked.

"I waited for them to answer. After an uncomfortable silence, Gregson finally broke out of his reticence and offered that one could go out and try to sell the flowers. Lestrade got into it immediately and objected that this wouldn't work, because both he and his 'old woman' already had too much to do to go out trying to sell flowers, and he knew the same went for Gregson. Gregson then said one could leave the house with the flowers, give them to a passerby and return with money in one's hand. You'd be out nothing, because the old man would give it back as his bit for the household. Lestrade agreed that this would answer his objection, but he thought the transaction should be made more real for dear old Granddad. The old man should see a real person pay for the flowers. They both then began to talk at the same time and ended up putting forth the same solution to the problem. Some third party would have to be brought into the deception who would call for the flowers and pay for them right before grandfather's eyes."

Watson couldn't hold himself back and laughed aloud and I joined him.

"Yes, I couldn't believe my little stratagem of presenting them with this problem of the imaginary grandfather would work so well. I had but to say, 'That, gentlemen, is the exact reasoning which the Home Secretary, Dr. Watson and I followed. Like the two of you, we realized that we needed to introduce the symbol of certain reality into our scheme. That symbol must consist of you two gentlemen and a real case for Sherlock Holmes to solve.'"

"And, after that?" Watson asked.

"Well, they were safely on board. They are bright men and when given a problem, were eager to sink their teeth into it. Immediately they pointed out that it would be an encumbrance to have an amateur underfoot while going about the serious effort to gather and process material evidence. Also, after a little hesitation, Lestrade admitted that he didn't like the idea of this amateur happening to stumble on a solution for which he would take credit. I hastened to assure them that in the unlikely event such a thing should happen we would make sure the credit for the successful wrapping-up of any case, as far as the press was concerned, would go to the two of them.

"Gregson then opined we had a problem with establishing the very note of reality brought up in the grandfather case, since no one would believe the police really needed to consult an amateur like Holmes. He added that not even a crazy man could believe such nonsense. I answered that as far as the general public was concerned he was undoubtedly correct, but Sherlock Holmes's egoism was such that he would never have any doubts that it was perfectly reasonable—in fact the *only* reasonable course for the police to follow.

"Understand, John, this discussion was decidedly in the spirit of problem solving, endeavoring to iron out the wrinkles in our little masque. Finally the two inspectors decided that, at least for the first instance, they would try to find a situation that could be made to give Sherlock the impression he was investigating while leaving no chance they could be faulted for risking the public's safety. This would also give them both an opportunity to get accustomed to the exercise in a trial run.

"I had to agree with them, although I believe none of us knew exactly what this really meant."

Watson sipped his tea while thinking about what he'd just heard. At length he said, "At any rate my dear fellow, you have managed to assemble your therapeutic team: Dr. Brandon Neal, Dr. John Watson, Inspectors Lestrade and Gregson and, behind the scene, Mycroft Holmes and the Home Secretary."

Thursday, March 3rd.

The tearoom at Fortnum & Mason was the chosen venue for our next meeting, being a reasonable distance for each of us, and a destination not likely to arouse Sherlock Holmes's suspicion, since John frequented the store, seeking interesting items in the food halls for the table at 221B Baker Street. Watson's scheme was to peruse the delicacies until he was sure he had not been followed.

I was already at a table and rose to shake his hand.

"I noticed you scanning the room, and I'm sure it wasn't in order to discover me."

John sat down and threw his napkin across his lap. "It's his habit of assuming outlandish disguises that keeps me on edge. I'm sure he didn't follow me here," he laughed, "but then what about that old lady walking on the opposite sidewalk? Seriously, Brandon, I'm sure he didn't follow me today. I watched him leave in a hansom then I legged it in the opposite direction. But you're right, keeping an eye out for him has become a constant reflex."

"Ah, here he comes now," I joked as a waitress approached our table.

John jumped, startled. "I say, you gave me a start!" he said laughing. "Sherlock is certainly capable of matching her appearance, but not her sweetness."

The mood had been set for a pleasant bit of conspiracy.

"And how is our patient? It has been over two weeks since we've talked—two weeks waiting for Lestrade and Gregson to come up with a 'case.'"

"Do you suppose they've changed their minds?"

"I don't know. I hope not."

"Anyway, Holmes is off to the laboratory at the hospital most days," John answered. "Incredible energy. But then for two full days he laid around our sitting room smoking, scraping at his violin and occasionally chuckling to himself, as if I were not in the room. At odd times he asked me to retire to my room so he could interview a client. I've sneaked a peek at these people: a well dressed man with the bearing of authority, a young woman like one who might wait on you in a glove shop, a ragamuffin of no more than eight and so on. And then there is his talking about the Mormons of Utah."

"Tell me about that."

"It seems he has done much reading about the sect. At the dinner table he will suddenly give a chuckle or snort and begin relating part of the story to me in a fashion as if I knew completely what he was taking about. As if everyone should know what he's talking about. It's the same story each time with additions. A young girl almost dies of thirst in the desert before she and an old male companion are rescued by a band of Mormons, who are traveling on their way to Utah. The girl grows to womanhood and falls in love with a young non-Mormon named Jefferson Hope.

"I thought at first that it was a story he had read, but I have come to believe he makes it up. It is so real to him that he talks about the characters as if they are real people."

"Fascinating." I have had considerable experience with delusions but nothing exactly like this. "How fortunate we are to have you there to observe and record all of this."

"Indeed," Watson affirmed. "But let me tell you the rest of the story. I feel I have a need to unload the weight of it," he said in an apologetic tone.

"I'm listening," I said.

"As I said, the young woman falls in love with a

virile young man, Jefferson Hope, passing through on his way to make his fortune in the California gold fields." Watson added, laughing, "Holmes even includes the irrelevant detail that the man was named after Thomas Jefferson. Anyway, before he can return and claim the girl, the Mormon elders decreed that she must marry one of them and forces the marriage upon her."

"Just a moment John, before you continue: What is Sherlock's mood while he is relating the story?"

"Ah yes, let's see, but first let me finish the story by saying briefly—although Sherlock's version is certainly not brief—that the dear young girl dies of a broken heart.

"Now then, his mood. He's very emotional, the emotion depending on the action in the story. He is outraged by the demands of the elders. And now that I think of it, there is one odd thing that happens: If I interrupt to ask for any clarification, he breaks off as if I were intruding into something private."

"Well observed, my friend. This is a classic description of the secretiveness of paranoia. What he related to you was a well-organized delusion. Although it is natural for you to think *you* are being told a story, in truth this is not so. As you said, he acted as if you already knew the story, or even that you were not there. If you interrupt with a question, you make your presence known and thus become an unwelcome intruder. If you witness a man hallucinating—talking actively to someone who isn't there—and you approach and ask him to whom he is speaking, he will immediately become silent. "

"Do you think, then, this suggests a worsening of his condition?"

"I don't think we can come to that conclusion. He may have been behaving thusly for some time. I believe I remember his brother, Mycroft, complaining about Sherlock going on and on about one obsession following another and that he was tired of hearing about the Mormons. But didn't you say there was something else you regarded as ominous?"

"Ah, yes," Watson answered. "The other night I was getting ready to retire for the evening and had turned off the lamp in my room when I noticed that my door was ajar. Light was coming through the crack from a lamp on Sherlock's desk. I went to the door to close it and chanced to see him bending over while doing something to his arm. When he had finished, I noticed that he put some object into the desk drawer. He always locks the drawer, but I saw that this time he went to his room leaving the drawer unlocked. I waited until I thought he'd be asleep and crept out of my room to have a look. I struck a match and opened the drawer. Inside lay a syringe and a phial of what must be cocaine. Brandon, his brother's suspicions are true. He is injecting himself."

I sat back and exhaled a long breath. "I don't mind telling you I don't like this a bit."

Watson nodded. "If only Lestrade and Gregson would come up with a case for Holmes. He may lay off the drug if he is stimulated by the role of star detective."

"Very likely. If I hear nothing from those two today, I'll contact Mycroft tomorrow and have him goad them into action."

That Evening

I had just put the kettle on the gas stove in my flat's small kitchen for a late cup of tea, when there was a knock on my door. It was nine p.m. Who could it be at this late hour? Watson was to come to my flat only as a last resort, and when I had seen him earlier in the day, there had been no hint of an impending emergency.

The last person I expected to see when I opened the door was Inspector Lestrade, yet there he stood with his hat in his hand.

"I'm sorry to bother you at this hour Dr. Neal, but Gregson and I have agreed that we have come upon an incident which may serve the purpose you gentlemen have in mind—to give Mr. Sherlock Holmes a real case."

I asked him to step inside, and took his hat and placed it on the hall table before leading him into the sitting room, anxious to hear more.

"Have a seat, Inspector," I said, "and tell me what you've come up with."

He took out his notebook and while searching for the relevant page, began, "I shouldn't call it a case, actually." He cleared his throat and his voice took on a tone and cadence as if he were making a report to a superior. "At approximately seven o'clock this evening we were notified of a death having occurred at number 3 Lauriston Gardens."

He looked up and added informally, "That's just off the Brixton Road."

He then went on with his presentation while consulting his notes. "Mr. James Brock, the owner of the estates agents firm of the same name, contacted the local constable to report that a Mr. Enoch Drebber, an American client, had fallen over dead while Brock was showing him this vacant property—that is the property at number 3 Lauriston Gardens. Mr. Drebber comes to England regularly to buy antiques, which he ships back to America to sell. He needed a location to store the items until he had a proper quantity to make up a shipment. Mr. Brock thought the property at 3 Lauriston Gardens was ideal for Drebber's need. Mr. Brock, who is subject to having nosebleeds, happened to suffer one while he was showing Mr. Drebber about the house. This Drebber became very excited, apparently frightened at the sight of blood, and suddenly clutched his chest and fell over backward."

Lestrade then said empathically, "The poor fellow had a deuce of a time trying to control his nosebleed while attempting to examine his client to determine the severity of the man's condition, while all the time being careful not to get blood on the fellow's clothes. Costly looking clothes they are at that. At any rate, when Brock determined that the situation was grave, he ran out to seek a constable in the next road."

He looked at me for my reaction.

"I see," I said. "And what is there about this incident which leads you and Gregson to think it a possible case for Sherlock Holmes?"

"Don't you see, sir, it's the blood. We tell Mr. Holmes that we have a case of death where there is no evidence of violence and yet there is an abundance of blood in the room – in a room in an abandoned house.

The fact that the 'victim' is an American adds to the mystery."

He searched my face for the approval he expected to see.

As I considered what I'd just heard, a smile gradually spread across my face. "Splendid, Inspector! Yes, a man is discovered in an abandoned house . . . blood . . . no known cause of death. But wait. A postmortem examination will have to be done —correct?"

"Why, yes."

"At that time it will be determined that the American probably died of a coronary thrombosis—and with that, the case will come to a close." Disappointment had replaced my exuberance.

"I presume the dead man is still in the house," I said.

"That's right, sir. Nothing has been touched except in the most minor way to establish that the man was dead."

At first blush, the idea that Lestrade had put forth—a case of death without signs of violence where there is also a great deal of blood—presented a problem worthy of Lestrade's seeking consultation with the "world's first consulting detective." But wouldn't Holmes very quickly conclude, just as I had, that the man had died of a natural cause, one not requiring his skill and, therefore, not serving our wish to bolster that identity.

On the other hand, maybe the case had possibilities—if embellished.

Lestrade, uncomfortable with my silent rumination, began flipping through the pages of his notebook.

Finally I said, "Inspector, I think you can see that in order for this case to serve to support Mr. Holmes's belief that he is a great detective, it can't end with a diagnosis of common heart ailment. It must seem to be a case of murder. He would be satisfied with no less. There being no evidence of physical violence, Holmes may consider a natural cause of death just as we have. But the absence of physical evidence of foul play, still permits murder having been committed—murder by poisoning. If we were to put some substance on the dead man's lips – something with an unpleasant odor – just enough for Holmes to detect."

Lestrade looked doubtful.

I hurried to state, "The substance could be completely removed before the body was taken to the morgue. It need not contaminate the actual autopsy examination."

Lestrade continued to think about it. He was already involved in such a deviation from standard protocol that his head was swimming. To actually tamper with evidence was close to original sin. He ran a finger between his tight collar and his bulging neck.

"Well, I don't know, sir. I'm worried about how far . . ."

"The medical examiner need never know."

Lestrade thought about the proposition. I knew what he was weighing in his mind – possible scandal vs. the indebtedness he might accrue with the Home Secretary.

"If ridding the corpse of the odor of this substance can be done up right . . . then there should be no harm," he said at last.

"No problem at all," I said confidently. "Now, what substance can we use?" Thinking aloud I said, "I wish I could get my hands on some prussic acid, but at this hour . . . At any rate the substance we use should have a sharp odor and it must be unfamiliar to Holmes."

A memory of coming into the kitchen when my housekeeper was polishing a silver teapot came to mind.

"She said the polish was a new brand," I said, puzzling Lestrade, I'm sure. "A new brand means he's less likely to identify it as metal polish. Come along," I said, leading the way into the kitchen where the tea kettle had just begun to sing.

I rummaged through the cleaning supplies in the cupboard under the sink.

"Here it is," I announced and stood up and removed the top from the tin of polish and sniffed cautiously. I thrust the tin under Lestrade's nose. "Recognize this smell?"

"Can't say that I do," he said frowning.

"Neither do I, but it is pungent enough to say it means business. It is certainly unlike the brand of polish one can find in most households. It's not prussic acid, but it will have to do. Let me fetch my coat and we can be off."

A thick pea-soup fog drifting up from the Thames slowed our journey. The driver of the police four-wheeler almost had to feel his way along Regent Street toward Westminster Bridge. Other carriages loomed up suddenly causing near collisions, which called forth oaths between the drivers. The fog seemed even denser south of the river along Kennington Road. At length, the driver pulled to the kerb, and Lestrade and I climbed down from the carriage. The house was actually on the Brixton Road, one of four set back some thirty feet from the street. Two of the houses were occupied, light showing through curtained windows, and two stood empty, their dark, blank facades promising nothing good to anyone daring to enter them. Number 3 was one of them. A "To Let" sign leaned against the pane of one of the dirty downstairs windows.

With a bulls-eye lamp extended in front of him, a constable came toward us as we passed through the gate and led us through the overgrown front yard, flooded from an earlier rainfall, to the front door.

The smell of damp neglect greeted us when we crossed the threshold of the foyer. A dark hallway extended from that room toward the rear of the house, where a wavering light shined into the hall. This light, a lantern, appeared and advanced toward Lestrade and me. Materializing above the lantern's glow like the ghost of Hamlet's father was the broad face of Inspector Gregson.

"Good evening, Doctor. Very glad you're here. I'll be happy indeed to get on with this business and get out of this dreary place. The body's this way in the dining room. Mind you don't step in all the blood."

He swung the lantern from side to side, illuminating the many splotches of blood on the floor, especially numerous at one side of the body of a man lying sprawled upon his back. The dead man looked middle-aged. He wore a frock coat and waistcoat. The collar and cuffs of his shirt were immaculate and the top hat lying beside him was well brushed.

From Lestrade's description of the man's final moments, I was inclined to conclude he had in fact died of an acute coronary thrombosis. The contorted expression of agony on the face reflected severe anginal pain—or the pain associated with the ingestion of certain poisons. So far so good. I leaned over and took one of the man's hands in mine and bent the fingers. There was only slight resistance: rigor had only begun. The death probably occurred two or three hours ago as reported.

I shot Lestrade a look which carried the prearranged message that he should lead Gregson and the constable out of the room, giving me the moment I needed to paint the inside of the man's lip with the silver polish solution. The three would be able to claim afterward that they witnessed no tampering with the corpse. I applied the false poison and took up the lantern and began looking about the room. It was empty of furnishings or pictures. Peeling, garish wallpaper covered the walls. In addition to the blood splatters, there were many footprints in the thick dust on the floor. Satisfied there was nothing more to be done in the room, I crossed the hall to join the others in the parlor.

"Anything of note in this room?" I asked.

"Not a thing except the footprints of the estate

agent and the dead man as they looked over the house," answered Gregson.

The candle I had seen from the street was in a holder on the fireplace mantle. It cast its light on the adjacent wall causing a yellowed patch of plaster exposed by the peeling wallpaper to stand out. The blank space caught my eye—and my imagination.

"Gentlemen, I think a theatrical touch is called for, something for the great detective to sink his teeth into. Since this is not really a criminal case, I don't suppose it would do any harm to write a word here on the wall."

"And what would that be, sir?" Lestrade asked.

"I'm not sure, but something which would stimulate his imagination."

I saw that the idea of playing a trick on Sherlock appealed to both inspectors, rankled as they both had been with his past haughty dealings with them.

Lestrade suggested, "Why not send him after foreign spies. He went on about them when I went to 'consult' him about tropical poisons. He had it that the spies were all about and the police were doing nothing."

"Nah," objected Gregson. "It were best if a woman were mixed up in the murder."

"Cherchez la femme is it?" I said. I looked at

Lestrade.

"Gregson's got a point," he returned.

"A woman it is, then," I said.

I returned to the dead man's side and, selecting a thick blob of blood that was still somewhat liquid near its base, I dipped my finger and returned to the plaster patch, where I wrote a capital 'R', intending to write Ruth, since it was short and the supply of liquid blood was scanty.

"Hah, the doctor's got your missus in mind, Gregson. Rachel."

Gregson joined his laughter and nodded agreeably. So I wrote the "a" then returned to the dining room to gather another dab of gory paint. With this, I managed "c, h and e" before my finger was dry. I wasn't sure I'd be able to find more liquid blood, but Lestrade spoke up.

"Let's leave it like that. Having to figure out that it was meant to spell Rachel gives Holmes one more thing to solve."

"Fair enough," I replied. "I think we're ready to bring Sherlock and introduce him to his case. But first we should run through the story he's to be told."

Lestrade looked at his partner, who cleared his throat. "Lestrade and I were thinking we'd ask him to come and give us his opinion about a case that was puzzling us. A constable saw a candle burning in a house that had stood empty for some time and investigated and discovered the body of a man. He has been identified by the papers he had on him as an American named Enoch Drebber of Cleveland in the United States of America. We were at a loss to explain all the blood while the body appeared to be unharmed. That's about the lot of it. We'd stand back and let him make of it what he would."

I said, "Excellent gentlemen. Keep it simple. I see one problem and it's this: Holmes will want to interview the constable who discovered the body. We will have to include one of your trusted men in the scheme, one who can spin a yarn while keeping a straight face."

Both inspectors turned as one to look toward the constable who had met Lestrade and me when we'd arrived and who was now standing by the fireplace.

Lestrade laughed. "There's the man, Doctor, John Rance."

Gregson added, "Next month John here is to join us as a detective inspector. There is no man on the entire force who can pull your leg with a straight face better than this man."

I caught Lestrade's eye with a glance, which he understood. Could Rance be trusted to be a member of the team? Might he fear that he could lose his hard won promotion if things went wrong? Or, would he realize that his security reached as high as the the Home Secretary?

Lestrade looked me steadily in the eyes and nodded.

I turned to John Rance and smiled. "I'm pretty sure Sherlock Holmes will contact you. Initially he'll try to impress you with his powers of observation. For instance, he may point out something about yourself, which it would seem impossible for him to know. The easiest way to convince him that you are genuine is to be naively impressed with what he says."

"I see, put 'im on a bit is it?"

"Yes, but don't say more than you need to, only the story Inspector Lestrade just reviewed. Make no mistake, you'll be dealing with a very brilliant and perceptive man."

Lestrade accompanied me to the waiting police conveyance that would take me back to my flat. With my foot on the step of the carriage, I turned to him. "After Sherlock Holmes leaves the scene, a little soap and water should take care of that silver polish in his mouth."

As the carriage started off, I immediately thought of John Watson and how I would have liked to have had the opportunity to alert him to what was about to take place as the inspectors brought Holmes in on the "case."

There was no way to do this at this hour. Then I began to think that it was perhaps for the best from Watson's position to know nothing and experience the kind of surprise Holmes would discern as normal.

Following Morning – Friday, 4th. March

The morning of March 4th was foggy. John Watson looked out of one of the two windows at 221B Baker Street at the dun colored veil that hung low over the opposite buildings. He had arisen late, but found that Sherlock was still eating breakfast. He rang for the house-keeper to prepare coffee and toast, sat down at the table with Holmes and picked up a magazine. Watson was rethinking the report he had given me the day before at Fortnum & Mason. Perhaps he had been unfair to his suite-mate. Holmes had his odd moments, but they were ones Watson would normally have overlooked, having acquired a socially attuned tolerance for his fellow man—a valuable trait in the military life—and would not normally have reported the kind of peccadillos he had apprised me of. But, he reminded himself, he was really not there to share digs, but as an observing physician.

Watson put down the magazine and glanced out the window where, across Baker Street, he noticed a husky, plainly dressed man carrying a large blue envelope walking along and looking anxiously at each house number.

"I wonder what that fellow is looking for?" he said to Holmes, pointing.

Holmes rose part way in order to see the person in question. "You mean the retired sergeant of the Marines?"

"What?" Watson muttered. But before he could inquire about Sherlock's surprising statement, he saw the man in question catch sight of 221B and run across the road.

Moments later there was a knock heard at the front door followed by heavy footsteps on the stair.

"For Mr. Sherlock Holmes," the fellow said, stepping into the room and holding out the blue envelope.

Watson couldn't believe that Holmes had been able to discern the man's former role in the military, including his rank, at a mere glance and wanted to check it out, but he also knew he mustn't do anything to undermine Holmes's notion that he possessed a remarkable capacity for such exceptional perspicacity. He couldn't restrain himself, however, from determining the truth of it.

"I say," he ventured as the man was handing over the envelope to Holmes. "You've not always been a messenger have you?"

"That's right, gov'nor, I was a sergeant in the Marine Light Infantry."

He clicked his heels together, raised his hand in salute and left the room.

"How on earth did you deduce that?" Watson asked in awe.

"Deduce what?" Holmes replied petulantly.

"Why, that he was a sergeant of the Marines."

Opening the letter, Holmes replied distractedly, "I have no time for trifles," and then began to read aloud.

"Dear Mr. Sherlock Holmes,

There has been a bad business during the night at 3 Lauriston Gardens, off the Brixton Road. Our man on the beat saw a light there about two in the morning and, as the house is an empty one, suspected that something was amiss. He found the door open and in the front room, which was bare of furniture, discovered

the body of a gentleman, well dressed and having cards in his pocket bearing the name of Enoch J. Drebber, Cleveland, Ohio, U.S.A.

There had been no robbery, nor is there any evidence as to how the man met his death. There are marks of blood in the room, but there is no wound upon his person. We are at a loss as to how he came into the empty house; indeed, the whole affair is a puzzler. If you can come round to the house any time before twelve, you will find me there. I left everything in statu quo until I hear from you. If you are unable to come, I shall give you fuller details, and would esteem it a great kindness if you would favour me with your reply.

Yours, faithfully,
Tobias Gregson"

"Gregson is the smartest of the Scotland Yarders," remarked Holmes, smiling with great satisfaction. "He and Lestrade are the pick of a bad lot. They are both quick and energetic, but conventional—shockingly so. They have their knives into one another, too. They are as jealous as a pair of professional beauties. There will be some fun over this case if they are both put on the scent."

So it had happened, thought Watson; the two detectives had found an incident upon which they felt safe to loose "the world's greatest detective." Watson was excited. The game was afoot.

"Surely there is not a moment to be lost," Watson cried. "Shall I go and order you a cab?"

"I'm not sure about whether I shall go. I am the most incurably lazy devil that ever stood in shoe leather," Holmes replied.

What have we here, wondered Watson. Was this the defensive retreat of a braggart when called to deliver on his boast? I could lift that horse if I wanted to, I just don't want to. If this was the case, then the plan was defeated. How could Sherlock's delusion be supported, if he was reluctant to be led into the play?

Watson realized he must be very careful of what he said. To pressure Holmes to respond to Gregson's letter might reveal his motives and unmask the plan at its outset. On the other hand, if Holmes did not go to the "crime" scene that the Scotland Yarders had staged, they would surely experience the whole charade as a gross waste of their time and cease to be participants.

Watson picked up the magazine and opened it while saying in an offhand manner, "Still, it seems to be a real puzzler, one in which I would have thought you would delight in exercising your skill."

"My dear fellow, what does it matter to me?

Supposing I unravel the whole matter? You may be sure that Gregson, Lestrade and company will pocket all the credit."

"But he begs you to help him."

"Yes. He knows that I am his superior, and acknowledges it to me; but he would cut his tongue out before he would own it to any third person. However, we may as well go and have a look. I shall work it out on my own hook. I may have a laugh at them, if I have nothing else. Come on!"

A wave of relief passed over Watson. The plan was still alive and judging by the way Holmes was hustling into his overcoat, a fit of energy had seized him.

"Get your hat," Holmes said urgently.

"You wish me to come?"

"Yes, if you have nothing better to do."

Soon they were hurrying along in a hansom cab toward the Brixton Road. Holmes was in high spirits, prattling away about violins and the differences between Stradivarius and Amati fiddles.

"You don't seem to give too much thought to the business at hand," Watson ventured.

"No data yet," Holmes answered. "It's a capital mistake to theorize before you have all the evidence. Biases your judgment."

Brixton Road was dreary, the buildings along its course shabby. If it weren't for the importance of this undertaking, Watson would have much preferred to be still in the cozy sitting room of 221B enjoying a good pipe and a newspaper. Holmes was staring out the window, lost in thought.

Watson broke the silence. "Since we have a few minutes before we come to Lauriston Gardens, perhaps you would tell me how you managed, with but a glance out the window, to know the messenger had been in the Marines."

"What's that? Oh, the ex-sergeant. It was simple really. A sudden, overall impression. I could see from across the road the giant blue tattooed anchor on the back of his hand. He had a military bearing and regulation side-whiskers. There we have the Marine. He displayed an air of self-importance, of command, hence the sergeant. His age—retired. It was all there for anyone to see . . . even you, my good friend."

Watson may have taken offense at the patent jibe in Holmes's last sentence, but he was already seeing him as his patient and therefore someone to be understood instead of responded to as one might in a normal social setting. And, as he had been in long habit of doing with patients, he reached into his coat pocket for the notebook he had carried with him for years and began to make a note, a note to be reported later to me.

"What are you doing?" Holmes sharply demanded.

Watson suddenly felt as if he had been caught in a foolish lapse of judgment, a lapse which might have given away the plan and betrayed the trust Mycroft and I had placed in him.

"Ah, I . . . uh . . . was going to make a note of the train of thought by which you arrived at your deduction. Your method fascinates me and if you would not find it offensive, I should like to put it together as . . . as a journal of this case."

Watson watched Holmes's face closely for a clue to his reaction to his extemporaneous answer. Holmes did not seem pleased. He frowned, pursed his lips. He emitted a sudden bark of a laugh.

"Yes. A journal. And why not? Why not indeed!"

Although Watson had only spoken of writing a journal as a spur-of-the-moment answer to Holmes's challenge, he began to entertain the idea that such a journal could play a part in our overall treatment plan.

Watson had only a moment to give thought to the journal idea before Holmes shouted to the driver to stop.

"The house is just up ahead. We'll walk from here, walk and see what we shall see."

Watson followed him and made a point of closely observing his behavior with a clinical eye. Instead of proceeding directly to the entrance of the house, Holmes lounged up and down in front of it with an air of nonchalance which, under the circumstances, Watson thought bordered on affectation. Holmes gazed vacantly at the ground, the sky and the surrounding buildings. He then made his way along the fringe of the grass, which flanked the path leading to the house. Minutely he studied the ground, emitting little sounds of satisfaction.

There were so many footprints in the soft soil made by the police that Watson couldn't see how Holmes could make anything of value out of what was to be seen there.

At the front door a tall, white-faced, blond man with notebook in hand rushed forward and clasped Holmes's hand exclaiming, "It is indeed kind of you to come. Everything is left untouched."

Pointing to the trampled path, Holmes remarked, "Except that, if a herd of buffaloes had passed along there, it could not be a greater mess. No doubt, however, you had drawn your own conclusions, Gregson, before you permitted this."

"I have had so much to do inside the house."

Holmes glanced at Dr. Watson and raised his

brows sardonically. "With two men like you and Lestrade in charge, there will not be much for me to find out."

The sarcasm was not lost on Gregson, but Watson saw him force back a rejoinder in kind.

"You didn't happen to come here in a cab?" Holmes asked.

"No, Lestrade and I came in a police conveyance. He's inside."

Holmes strode imperiously past Gregson. "Then let's go and look at the room."

Watson followed him into a bare, damp room. Immediately his attention was drawn to the lifeless figure lying on its back in the center of the floor. He watched Holmes kneel and examine the body intently.

"You are sure there is no wound?" he said.

"Positive," cried both detectives.

"Then, of course this blood belongs to a second individual—presumably the murderer—if murder has been committed. It reminds me of the circumstances attendant on the death of Van Jansen in Utrecht, in 1834. Do you remember the case, Gregson?"

"No, sir."

"Read it up. You really should. There is nothing new under the sun. It has all been done before."

Sherlock's fingers had been busy going over the

body and the man's clothes. Finally he smelled the man's lips.

Getting up, he announced, "You can take him to the mortuary now. There is nothing more to be learned."

Gregson called a couple of men to bring the stretcher. As they lifted the body onto it, a ring tinkled down and rolled across the floor. Gregson grabbed it up and stared at it with mystification.

"There's been a woman here," he cried. "It's a woman's wedding ring."

"This complicates matters," said Gregson.

"Are you sure it doesn't simplify them?" observed Holmes. "At any rate, there's nothing to be learned by staring at it. Did you find anything in his pockets?"

Gregson pointed to a pile on the bottom step of the stair. "Gold watch, chain, gold ring with a Masonic device, gold pin with a bulldog's head, a card-case and a handkerchief with the initials E.J.D. That matches the name on the cards in the case, Enoch J. Drebber of Cleveland. Also, there was a pocket edition of Boccaccio's Decameron with the name Joseph Stangerson on the fly-leaf and two letters, one addressed to Drebber and the other to Stangerson."

"At what address?"

"American Exchange, Strand. They are both from

the Guion Steamship Company and refer to the sailing of their boats from Liverpool. It is clear that this unfortunate man was about to return to New York."

"Have you made inquiries about this man Stangerson?"

"Yes, but we have no information yet."

"Have you sent to Cleveland?"

"We telegraphed this morning."

"How did you word your inquiry?"

"We gave the details and asked for any information which could help us."

"You did not ask for any particulars on any point which appeared to you to be crucial?"

"I asked about Stangerson."

"Nothing else? Is there no circumstance upon which this case hinges?" The note of incredulity couldn't be missed by anyone present.

Watson was afraid Gregson had taken as much as he could from Holmes and would reply in a way that would endanger the plan, but at that very moment Lestrade stuck his head in the room and announced excitedly, "Come here!" and led them all into the neighboring room.

"Look at that," he said pointing to an area of bare plaster on the wall near the fireplace.

Across the space was scrawled the word, "Rache", in blood red letters.

"What do you think it means?" asked Gregson.

Lestrade answered him, "Why, it's certainly blood. The murderer was using some of the blood round about on the floor to write the name Rachel, but was disturbed before he could finish."

Sherlock Holmes burst out laughing.

Watson was sure that this insult would undo any resolve the two detectives had about staying the course. He was relieved to hear Holmes begin an apology.

"I really beg your pardon. You certainly have the credit of being the first to find this out."

As he spoke, he took a tape measure and a large round magnifying glass out of his pocket. For the next several minutes he trotted noiselessly around the room taking measurements, kneeling and at one point he actually lay face down on the floor. All the while he kept chattering to himself. Watson was reminded of a foxhound finding, then losing, then once again finding the scent. At one point Sherlock gathered up a little pile of gray dust from the floor and put it in a small envelope. Lastly, he examined the bloody letters on the wall minutely with his glass. The two inspectors, watching this performance, gave each other knowing looks and Lestrade chanced a quick wink at Watson.

Holmes, apparently satisfied, returned the tape measure to his pocket. "They say that genius is the infinite capacity for taking pains. It's a very bad definition, but it does apply to detective work."

"What do you make of all this, sir?" they asked together.

"It would be robbing you of the credit of the case if I was to presume to help you. You are doing so well now it would be a pity for anyone to interfere."

The sarcasm of the remark hung over the small group like a storm cloud.

"But, if you let me know how your investigations go," he continued, "I shall be happy to give you any help I can. In the meantime I should like to speak to the constable who found the body. Can you give me his name and address?"

Lestrade was ready with the address, but he pretended to consult his notebook. "John Rance. He's off duty now. You'll find him at 46, Audley Court, Kensington Park Gate."

"Come along, Doctor, we shall look him up." He started to walk away and then stopped and turned back to the two detectives. "I'll tell you one thing which may help you in the case. There has been murder done and the murderer is a man. He was more than six feet tall, was in the prime of life, had small feet for his height, wore coarse, square-toed boots and smoked a Trichinopoly cigar. He came here with the victim in a four-wheeled cab, which was drawn by a horse with three old shoes and one new one on his fore off-leg. In all probability the murderer had a florid face. These are only a few of the indications, but they might assist you."

This was said in the tone of someone reeling off instructions for his maid as he left the house in the morning.

Lestrade and Gregson both looked overwhelmed— and they were not acting.

"If this man was murdered," the former asked. "How was it done?"

"Poison," Sherlock Holmes said curtly and strode off. At the door, he turned once again and added, "'Rache' is German for 'revenge', so don't lose your time looking for Miss Rachel."

All through the time at Lauriston Gardens Watson ached to know the details that lay behind the scene—how the detectives had staged it. Later, after he had related the scene at Lauriston Gardens to me, I was reassured that it had been a good decision to have not attempted to inform him, because it sounded like his reactions had been natural and convincing to Holmes.

It was one o'clock when Holmes and Watson left Lauriston Gardens and Holmes directed the cabman to take them to the nearest telegraph office where he dispatched a long telegram. This done, he gave the driver the address of Constable Rance.

"There is nothing like first-hand evidence," he remarked as they pulled away. "As a matter of fact, my mind is entirely made up upon the case, but still we may as well learn all that is to be learned."

"You amaze me, Holmes." Watson remarked. "Surely you can't be as positive as you pretend to be of all those particulars which you gave those men back there." By this time Watson had become so certain of the depth of Sherlock's notion of omnipotence that he knew that his mild challenge would not shake him.

"There's no room for mistake. The fact that it began raining during the night means the wheel ruts I observed were made after the rain. They were the wheels of a cab. The imprint of the horse's hooves was plain also. Since the police did not use a cab, it must have brought the two men there."

"I see, but what about the other man's height?"

"Why, the height of a man in nine cases out of ten can be told from the length of his stride."

"Ah, yes." Watson was thinking, however, that he had seen short men who strode out like Napoleon and tall men who took mincing steps.

"Also, I measured the distance from the wall-writing to the floor. A man tends to write at eye level and the writing was exactly six feet from the ground."

Watson reckoned it to be about five inches from the eyes to the top of the head. Six foot five would be tall indeed. He suspected that I had done the writing before he and Holmes arrived and I am only six feet tall.

"And the florid face?"

"It is only a full-blooded man who will have a nosebleed caused by emotion alone and, as you saw for yourself, there was no sign of a struggle, so it is unlikely the blood was a result of the murderer being injured."

"Ah ha, I see," Watson said. He was thinking that this conclusion was patently false. He had known many who suffered from spontaneous nosebleeds, who were slight of build and pale of complexion. "And what of the writing in blood?" he asked.

"Ah, that was a blind, my dear fellow—a blind to throw the police off the track. It was intended to suggest secret societies, socialism, but the writer was not German. If you noticed, the 'A' was printed somewhat after the German fashion, but a real German invariably prints in the Latin character. So, this was a clumsy imitator who overdid it. I don't want to tell you more about the case, Doctor. A conjurer gets no credit once he has explained his trick. If I show you too much of my method of working, you will conclude that I am a very ordinary individual after all."

Watson realized what his role in our plan called for. "I shall never do that," he answered. "You have brought detection to as near an exact science as it will ever be brought to in this world."

Watson noted the effect of his words. Holmes flushed with pleasure.

"I'll tell you one other thing. The two men came in the same cab. They walked up the path together as friendly as possible. Inside the house, the victim stood still while the murderer—who wore square-toed boots— walked about. His lengthening stride indicates that he was becoming excited. Then the tragedy occurred. We have a good working basis on which to start. We must hurry up, for I want to go to Halle's concert to hear Neruda this afternoon."

While they talked, the cab had been threading its way through dingy streets. In the dreariest of them, the cab stopped and the driver called down, "That's Audley Court in there."

He was pointing to a narrow slit in the line of dead-colored brick buildings.

"Wait for us here," said Holmes, climbing out of the cab and leading the way through the narrow passage into a courtyard surrounded by sordid dwellings. They made their way through lines of discolored linen and groups of dirty children up to Number 46. A small slip of brass on the door was engraved with the name Rance.

The woman who answered the door told them that the constable was still in bed. She showed them into a small parlor and asked them to wait.

At length Rance appeared, feigning sleepiness and appearing disgruntled at being disturbed.

Watson was struck by Holmes's failure to introduce himself, or inform the constable that his superiors had given us the constables address. Holmes's ego needed no introduction.

"I gave my report at the office," Rance said.

Holmes took a half-sovereign from his pocket and played with it pensively. "We thought we should like to hear it all from your own lips."

Watson hadn't been able, being unaware of what Rance had been coached to say, to appreciate how deftly the constable played his role. Rance eyed the gold disk avariciously. "I shall be most happy to tell you anything

I can."

"Just let us hear it all in your own way."

Rance sat down on the horsehair sofa and knitted his brow as though he were determined not to omit anything.

"I'll tell ye from the beginning." He then commenced to repeat the story the two detectives and I had rehearsed with him back at Lauriston Gardens. He masterfully embroidered it with appropriate color and irrelevant detours. At one point in the narrative, Sherlock Holmes couldn't resist the impulse to impress the constable with one of his flights of deduction and before Rance had a chance to describe it himself, told him what the constable had found upon first opening the door and entering the abandoned house.

John Rance sprang to his feet with a frightened face and suspicion in his eyes. "Where was you hid to see all that?" he cried. "It seems to me that you knows a great deal more than you should."

Rance would have been elevated to inspector status on the spot if only Lestrade and Gregson had been there to witness his performance.

Holmes, laughing, immediately identified himself as working with the police and gave him his card. Rance sat again, but still wore the expression of mystification.

He went on with the story he was told to relate, but was having so much pleasure in his acting that he decided to add a scene of his own invention.

"When I went outside to blow my whistle to bring help from the men on the surrounding beats, there were a drunk hanging over the front gate, singing to the top of his lungs about Columbine's New-fangled Banner, or some such stuff."

"Describe him," urged Holmes.

"He was pretty much muffled up, but I reckon him to be a long chap with a red face."

"That will do," cried Holmes. "What became of him?"

"We'd enough to do without looking after him. I'll wager he found his way home all right."

"How was he dressed?"

"In a brown overcoat."

"Had he a whip in his hand?"

"A whip? . . . No."

"He must have left it behind," Holmes muttered. "You didn't happen to see or hear a cab after that?"

"No."

"There's a half-sovereign for you," Holmes said and stood up. "I'm afraid, Rance, that you will never rise in the force. That head of yours should be made for use as well as ornament. You might have gained your sergeant stripes last night. The man whom you held in your hands is the man who holds the clue of this mystery, and whom we are seeking. Come along, Doctor."

Holmes got back into the cab and stared straight ahead, tense and angry. Watson, seeing that Sherlock was leaving the driver for him to deal with, gave the man their Baker Street address and climbed in beside Holmes.

"The blundering fool!" Holmes said bitterly. "Just to think of his having such an incomparable bit of luck, and not taking advantage of it."

Forgetting for a moment his role in the treatment plan, Watson was drawn into making an objection. "Hold on a moment, Holmes. I'm dashed confused. If this drunk was the second party in the house with the murdered man—and I grant you the constable's description matches the one you predicted—why would he come back to the house after leaving it? That's not the way of criminals."

Sherlock Holmes welcomed Watson's question. "The ring, man, the ring! That was what he came back for. If we have no other way of catching him, we can always bait our line with the ring. I shall have him, Doctor—I'll lay you two to one that I have him. I must thank you for it all. I might not have gone but for you, and so missed the finest study I ever came across: a study in scarlet, eh? Why shouldn't we use a little art jargon? There's a scarlet thread of murder running through the colorless skein of life, and our duty is to unravel it, and expose every inch of it. Now for lunch and then on to hear Neruda play. What's that little thing of Chopin's she plays so magnificently: Tra-la-la-lira-lira-lay."

Hypomania, Watson decided. But, the treatment plan seemed to be accomplishing the desired result. Sherlock Holmes was totally given over to the case. And if he did follow through with the idea of putting together a journal of this case, John Watson knew what he would call it: A Study in Scarlet.

The **Same Day - Afternoon**

Watson begged off from an afternoon with the violinist and got down from the cab alone at their lodgings as Holmes drove off. Watson immediately walked a half block to a tobacconist's shop, where he handed the young assistant a page torn from his notebook. On it he had written, "Holmes sent telegram from the exchange in Waterloo Station." Watson and I had hit upon that method as a safe way to pass messages between us, and the shop assistant was glad of the odd bit of change he picked up as a messenger.

After taking the message from Watson, the young man retrieved a sealed envelope from under his counter and handed it to him saying. "Not an hour ago, sir, a messenger brought this for you."

Watson opened the envelope and read, "Not murder. Coronary occlusion with stage props. The man was here with his secretary, named Stangerson. They are looking for him now to inform him of Drebber's death."

Watson smiled. He was relieved to be brought up to date.

I received Watson's message informing me of the telegram Holmes had sent and having no scheduled appointment for an hour, I hurried in a cab to pick up Lestrade and continue on to the telegraph office at Waterloo.

"Gregson got the answer to his telegram to the Cleveland Police Department only half an hour ago," Lestrade told me when the cab was under way. "It confirmed that Enoch Drebber was an antique dealer there who, according to his wife, has been in England for a month with his assistant buying antiques."

"As expected," I replied.

The manager of the telegraph exchange office where Sherlock Holmes sent his recent dispatch didn't turn a hair when Lestrade announced to him that he required to be shown the text of Holmes's telegram.

"Always happy to help the police."

We were handed the copy written by Holmes. It was addressed to the Cleveland Police Headquarters. Holmes had requested information about Enoch Drebber's *marriage*. That was all. Lestrade was just instructing the manager to notify him at Scotland Yard the moment a reply, if any, came for Sherlock Holmes, when the reply was received from America. The message was brief and to the point. "No unauthorized information concerning citizens is given out by the Cleveland Police Department."

I drew Lestrade aside. "We must substitute another message which will support Holmes's ideas," I whispered.

"Ah yes, of course . . . but what?"

"Dr. Watson has related to me the details of Holmes's fantasized story of intrigue in the Mormon community in Utah. I'd be willing to wager this inquiry of his about the American's marriage springs from that story. Holmes has been rambling on about Mormon elders separating two young lovers and forcing the girl to marry one of the elders. Holmes has even invented names for the lovers, Jefferson Hope and Lucy Ferrier. My hunch—and I admit it is no more than that—is that Holmes believes Enoch Drebber is the man Lucy was forced to marry and Jefferson Hope has followed him to London and murdered him."

"My dear Doctor Neal," replied Lestrade in disbelief, "That's going a bit far."

"Yes but delusions in a case such as this are not uncommon, and they can incorporate much odd detail."

"I say!"

"If I'm right about how Holmes has tied his delusions and Drebber's death together—and it is a bit of a gamble, I admit—then the telegram reply from Cleveland should contain information to support Holmes's line of thinking. In his own telegram, Holmes asked for information about Drebber's marriage. If I remember correctly what Dr. Watson told me, the young woman, Lucy, died of a broken heart."

"Then the telegram can say Drebber is a widower," suggested Lestrade.

"Right, but perhaps we can do more. We can say that Enoch Drebber had asked the Cleveland police for protection from a rival in love named Jefferson Hope, who is thought to be in Europe presently."

"Well now, sir, that's not something the police

would be likely to say in a telegram. Who would believe such a thing?"

"Sherlock Holmes."

Holmes returned late to his and Watson's rooms after the concert. Dinner was already on the table, curried mutton with rice for John and for Sherlock it was the mutton with his preferred parslied potatoes.

"It was magnificent," he exclaimed, pacing up and down the length of the sitting room, before finally taking his seat at the dinner table. "Darwin says that the power to produce and appreciate music was arrived at by us humans long before the possession of speech. This is, perhaps, why we are so influenced by it. There are memories in our souls of those misty centuries when the world was in its childhood."

So, Watson observed to himself, the mania continues.

"Have you seen the paper's evening edition?" asked Holmes, holding up a copy of his favorite, *The Echo*.

"No."

"It gives a fairly good account of the affair. No mention of murder, of course. Lestrade and Gregson are reluctant to face the truth, but they will when the post-mortem is performed. The article also does not mention a ring being found. Just as well it doesn't."

"Why?"

"Look at this advertisement," he answered. "I had it placed in all the papers before I went to the theater."

He threw the paper across to Watson and indicated the advertisement. It was the first entry in the "found" column.

"In Brixton Road, this morning, a plain gold wedding ring found in the roadway between the White Hart Tavern and Holland Grove. Apply Dr. Watson, 221B, Baker Street between eight and nine this evening."

"Excuse my using your name without your prior permission," Holmes offered perfunctorily, "If I used my own, some of these police dunderheads would recognize it and want to meddle in the affair."

Flagrant megalomania, Watson observed to himself as he said, "That's all right, but supposing anyone applies, I have no ring."

"Oh yes, you have," Holmes said, handing him a ring. "This will do very well. It is almost identical."

"And who do you expect to answer the ad?"

"Why, the man in the brown coat—our florid faced friend with the square toes. If he does not come himself, he will send an accomplice."

"Wouldn't he consider it too dangerous?"

"Not at all. This man would rather lose anything than lose the ring. He dropped it while bending over Drebber's body and did not miss it at the time. He discovered he no longer had it after leaving the house and came back for it, but he found that the police were already there—he met constable Rance at the gate and pretended to be drunk. What would he do then? Why, he would eagerly look in the evening paper in the 'found' column. He will come! We will see him within the hour."

"And then?" Watson asked.

"You can leave me to deal with him. Have you a gun?"

"I have an old army revolver and a few cartridges."

"You had better clean it and load it. He will be a desperate man."

Watson knew he had to play his part in this farce and do what Holmes ordered. No one, of course, would answer the notice Holmes had placed in *The Echo*.

A knock at the sitting room door fairly made Watson jump. Holmes quickly advanced to the door and opened it with a flourish. There stood a telegram delivery boy, who in turn was startled by the dramatic pose of the man who had flung open the door.

"T . . . T . . . Telegram for Mr. Sherlock Holmes,"

he stammered.

Holmes took the envelope from the boy, gave him a sixpence and closed the door. He ripped the envelope open and read it quickly.

"Ha, just as I thought. This is the answer to my American telegram. My view of the case is the correct one."

"And that is?" Watson asked eagerly.

"My fiddle would be the better for new strings," Holmes remarked, intentionally ignoring Watson's question. He sat and picked up the paper, remarking, "Put your pistol in your pocket. When the fellow comes, speak to him in an ordinary way. Leave the rest to me. Don't frighten him by looking at him too hard."

Saying this, Sherlock Holmes put down the paper and went to and opened the door slightly then walked to one of the windows and furtively looked down at the sidewalk. "Here comes our man I think."

As he spoke there was a sharp ring of the bell. Holmes moved a chair closer to the door and sat again. A servant was heard passing along the hall, then the click of the latch as she opened the front door.

"Does Dr. Watson live here?" asked a clear but rather harsh voice." Watson could not hear the reply, but he heard someone ascending the stair. It was an uncertain, shuffling step and a look of surprise passed over Sherlock's face. There followed a feeble tap at the door.

"Come in," Watson called out.

Instead of the violent murderer Holmes expected, a frail, wrinkled, old woman hobbled into the apartment. She seemed overwhelmed by the brightness of the room and stood there blinking for a moment before she dropped a curtsy.

Watson glanced at Holmes and saw such a dismal look on his face that it was all he could do to stifle a smile.

With fumbling fingers, the old woman drew a copy of *The Echo* out of a pocket of her coat. "It's this as has brought me, good gentlemen," she said dropping another curtsy. "A gold wedding ring in Brixton Road. It belongs to my girl Sally, as was married only this time twelve-month, which her husband is steward aboard a Union boat, and which he'd say if he come 'ome and found her without her ring is more than I can think, he being short enough at the best o' times, but more especially when he has the drink. If it please you, she went to the circus last night along with . . . "

Holmes seemed to be too disconsolate to move or speak, so Watson took over. "Is that her ring?" he said, and showed her the ring Holmes had purchased as bait for his trap.

"Lord be thanked!" the old woman cried. "Sally will be a glad woman this night. That's the ring."

"And what may your address be?" Watson asked taking up a pencil.

"13 Duncan Street, Houndsditch. A weary way from here."

"The Brixton Road does not lie between any circus and Houndsditch," Sherlock Holmes interjected sharply.

The woman turned to face Holmes and said submissively, "The gentleman asked me for my address. Sally lives in lodgings at 3, Mayfield Place, Peckham."

"And your name is . . . ?" demanded Holmes.

"My name is Sawyer. Hers is Dennis, which Tom Dennis married her, and a smart, clean lad, too, as long as he's at sea, and no steward in the company more thought of. But when he's on shore, what with the women and what with liquor shops . . . "

"Here is your ring," Watson interrupted, following a sign from Holmes. "It clearly belongs to your daughter, and I'm glad to be able to restore it to its rightful owner."

Watson knew that the woman had mistakenly identified the ring lost by her unfortunate daughter. Holmes was going to be out the price of a wedding band.

With mumblings of gratitude, the old woman put

it in her pocket and shuffled off down the stairs. The moment she was out the door, Sherlock Holmes sprang to his feet and ran to his room. He emerged moments later wearing his ulster and scarf.

"I'll follow her," he said. "She must be an accomplice, and will lead me to him. Wait up for me."

Watson went to the window and peered out onto Baker Street. Through the thickening fog, he could see the woman walking feebly along on the opposite sidewalk. Holmes had fallen in behind her at some distance. Watson was able now to focus on the meaning of the old woman coming to claim the ring. He had had to be very careful while she was in the apartment to appear to believe she was an accomplice of the murderer as Holmes did. Could it be that Brandon Neal and the police arranged for her to come and claim the ring? No, he decided, it was not likely they'd have spotted the advertisement Holmes placed in the paper. Who was she, then? She was certainly not the accomplice of a murderer. There had been no murder. She must be who she professed to be, a concerned mother making an effort to save her daughter a beating.

Watson filled a pipe, picked up Henri Muger's *Vie de Boheme* and settled down to wait. It was nine when Holmes set out; at ten Watson heard the maid pass down the hallway on the way to her room; at eleven it was the landlady's tread he heard. Shortly before twelve, Holmes's key turned in the latch.

One look told Watson that Holmes had failed in some way. Chagrin was written on his face. Then the beginnings of amusement began to show and finally take over as he burst into laughter.

"I wouldn't have Scotland Yard know it for the world." And here he gave Watson an admonitory look. "I've chaffed them so much they would never let me hear the end of it. I can afford to laugh, because I know that I will be even with them in the long run."

"What happened?"

Holmes took off his coat and hung it on the rack near the door, then dropped exhausted into a chair facing Watson. He sighed. "That creature had gone a little way when she began to limp, showing signs of being footsore. She stopped and waited until a four-wheeler came along and she hailed it. I happened to be close enough to hear the address." Holmes shook his head in acknowledgment of his obtuseness. "She sang it out so you could hear across the street, 'Drive to number 13, Duncan Street, Houndsditch.' Once she was inside, I perched on the back of the carriage—an art in which every detective should be expert – until, without a stop, we arrived at the address. I hopped off before the carriage came to a stop and began strolling down the walk in a casual way. The cab stopped, the driver got down and opened the door, but no one got out. When I walked up, he was swearing like a sailor and peering into his empty cab. When the driver and I inquired at number 13, we found that a respectable paperhanger lived there named Keswick. No one named Sawyer or Dennis had ever been heard of."

"You mean that tottering, old woman was able to leap from a moving cab?" Watson cried.

"Old woman be damned!" Sherlock replied. "We were the old women to be so taken in. It must have been a young man in a masterful disguise, an incomparable actor too. He knew he was being followed and gave me the slip. What it means is that the man we are after has friends ready to risk something for him. Now, Doctor, you are looking done-up. Take my advice and turn in."

John Watson retired to his room thinking about the egotism of a person who first tells you to wait up until midnight for his return and then advises you to turn in. As he disrobed in preparation for bed, he revised his conclusion about the old woman. Who was she, now that it was known that she was an impostor? John suspected that they—Holmes in particular—were the victims of a confidence artist, not a young man at all, but a woman old enough to feign aging decrepitude, yet still young enough to swing away from a moving cab. Answering advertisements in the "found" column must be her regular *modus operandi*.

Saturday, 5th. March

The morning papers were filled with the "Brixton Mystery", as they termed it. Watson snatched up one paper after another, wondering what had gone wrong. The plan was for this operation to be kept away from the awareness of the press. No doubt one of the constables couldn't pass up a five-bob bribe to tell a reporter a few details. A real murder, after all, calls for the police to come up with a real killer. Something had gone badly wrong and Watson feared the police would now be very sorry to have cooperated with us.

The *Daily Telegraph* said there had seldom been a crime with stranger features. The German name of the victim, the absence of all other motive and the sinister inscription on the wall, all point to political refugees and revolutionists. The socialists have branches in America and Drebber had undoubtedly violated their unwritten laws and had been tracked down by them.

The Standard opined that lawlessness like this usually occurred under a Liberal administration. This arose from the unsettling of the minds of the masses, and the consequent weakening of all authority. It reported a detail that caught Watson's attention. Drebber had been living in London for several weeks with his secretary, Mr. Joseph Stangerson, at the boarding house of Madame Charpentier in Torquay Terrace, Camberwell. The two left the boarding house on the third for Euston Station where they said they were to catch the Liverpool Express. They had, in fact, been seen together on the platform at Euston. The paper went on to say that it was encouraging that both Inspectors Lestrade and Gregson were on the case and, therefore, results could be expected shortly.

The Daily News revealed that the discovery of the boarding house address was through the excellent work of Inspector Gregson. They bemoaned the state of affairs on the continent, which had driven so many bitter men to England, men who live by their own harsh sense of justice.

Watson looked up from the paper to see a look of amusement on Sherlock's face. "I told you that whatever happened, Lestrade and Gregson would be sure to score."

"That depends on how it turns out."

"Oh bless you, it doesn't matter in the least. If the man is caught, it will be on account of their exertions; if he escapes, it will be in spite of their exertions. It's heads they win, tails I lose."

At this point Watson heard the pattering of many steps on the stair and the disgusted cries of the landlady.

"What on earth is going on?" Watson exclaimed.

"It's the Baker Street division of the police force," Holmes replied and at that instant the door burst open and a half dozen of the dirtiest ragamuffins clamored into the room.

"Ten-shun!" Holmes cried, and the six little scoundrels lined up in a caricature of a military review. "In the future," Holmes scolded, "You shall send Wiggins up alone to report, and the rest of you must wait in the street. Have you found it, Wiggins?"

"No sir, we hain't," replied the tallest boy.

"I hardly expected you would. You must keep on until you do. Here are your wages." He handed each of them a shilling. "Now, off you go and come back with a better report next time."

He waved his hand and they scattered like so many rats.

"There's more work to be got out of those little

beggars than out of a dozen on the force. The mere sight of an official looking person seals men's lips. These boys, however, go everywhere and hear everything. Sharp as needles too."

"Is it on the Brixton Road case that you are employing them?" Watson asked.

Holmes was at the window, having watched the departure of his detective squad. "Yes, there is a point which I wish to ascertain. Here, what have we here? It's Gregson headed this way with a beautiful smile. We're about to hear some news with a vengeance."

Heavy footsteps mounted the stairs, three at a time. Watson went to the door to open it for the detective.

Gregson strode in and faced Holmes. "My dear fellow," he fairly bellowed, "Congratulate me! I have made the whole thing as clear as day."

"You mean you're on the right track?" Holmes asked.

"Right track? Why I have the man under lock and key."

"And his name is?"

"Arthur Charpentier," exuded Gregson with pride.

Watson glanced at Holmes and saw him give a

sigh of relief and relax into a smile.

"Take a seat. Try one of these cigars. You'll have some whiskey won't you?"

"I don't mind if I do," said Gregson

"Now tell us how you managed it."

Watson wondered what the Scotland Yarders and I were up to. Things had obviously been moving too rapidly for us to keep him up to date.

"Ah, the exertions I've been through this day. Not physical as much as mental. You'll appreciate that Mr. Holmes, both of us being brain-workers."

"You do me too much honor," said Holmes gravely. "Let us hear how you arrived at this gratifying result."

Gregson was puffing away complacently on the cigar, then he suddenly slapped his thigh in amusement.

"The fun of it is that the fool Lestrade, who thinks himself so smart, has gone off on the wrong track altogether. He's after the secretary, Stangerson, who had no more to do with the crime than a babe unborn."

Here he laughed so hard he began to choke.

Holmes pressed him. "And how did you come upon your clue?"

"I'll tell you all about it." He snapped his head around to confront Watson. "Mind now, Doctor, this is strictly between ourselves."

"Yes, of course."

"First we had to find Drebber's American antecedents. Some people would have placed an advertisement and waited until someone came forward. That is not Tobias Gregson's way, no siree! You remember the hat beside the dead man?"

"Yes." Holmes answered, "By John Underwood and Sons, 129, Camberwell Road."

Gregson looked quite crestfallen. "I had no idea that you noticed that. Have you been to the shop?"

"No."

"Ha!" Gregson cried in a relieved voice; "You should never neglect a chance, however small it may seem."

"To a great mind, nothing is little," remarked Holmes sententiously, hardly attempting to hide his sarcasm.

"Well, I went there and discovered that the hat had been sold and delivered to a Mr. Drebber, residing at Charpentier's Boarding Establishment, Torquay Terrace."

"Smart—very smart," murmured Holmes.

"I went there. Madame Charpentier appeared to be very pale and I could see that her daughter, a comely miss, had been crying. I began to smell a rat. You know the feeling, Mr. Holmes, when you come upon the right scent—a kind of thrill in your nerves. I asked them if they had heard about Drebber's death and they had. They said that he and his secretary, Mr. Stangerson, had left their house at 8 p.m. on Thursday. Mr. Stangerson said they were taking the Liverpool Express, one train departing at 9:15 p.m. the other at 11:00 p.m.

"'And was that the last you saw of Drebber?' I asked. The mother was shaken by my question and stammered that it was the last time they had seen him, but I could tell she was lying. The girl said, 'No good can ever come of falsehood, Mother. We did see Mr. Drebber again.'"

Watson and Holmes then had to sit and listen to a lengthy description of how Gregson had skillfully elicited the entire story of how Drebber had been making amorous advances to the daughter all during his stay at the boarding house, culminating with a proposal of marriage when he returned alone after he and his secretary had left earlier for Euston Station. He claimed he was a rich man and the young girl would live with him in luxury in America. Upon her refusal, he grabbed her by the arm and tried to pull her out of the house. At this moment, the girl's brother, Arthur, a sailor in the navy, came into the room, took hold of Drebber and ejected him from the house. The young man got his hat and a walking stick and left after Drebber, saying, "I'll just go after him and see what he does with himself."

Gregson continued, "The last part of the story was told to me by the daughter amidst much sobbing. I could hardly hear her she spoke so low, but I managed to catch every word and I took complete notes."

"It's quite exciting," said Holmes, yawning. "What happened next?"

"I knew the entire case hung on one point, so fixing my eye in a way that is always effective with women, I asked when her brother returned home. 'I don't know' she said. 'He came home after we were in bed.'

"Well, after that there was nothing more to be done. I found out where Arthur Charpentier was and arrested him. When I did, he boldly said, 'I suppose you're arresting me for being connected with that scoundrel, Drebber.' As good as a confession, I'd say."

"Your theory, then?" put Sherlock Holmes as he slyly winked at Watson.

"He followed Drebber to Brixton Road where, being alone, he came up to him and hit him in the stomach with the walking stick, causing his death while leaving no trace. He saw the empty building, so he dragged the body inside. The blood, the writing on the wall and the ring were left to throw us off the scent."

Gregson looked first at Holmes and then Watson for the approval he expected. Watson thought to himself that Gregson's "theory" was so patently implausible that the inspectors and I must have hatched it as an example of police stupidity, giving Holmes proof of his own superior ability. If that were the case, Gregson was doing a splendid job.

"Well done," cried Holmes. "Really, Gregson, you *are* getting along. We shall make something of you yet. By the way, did the young man make a statement?"

"Yes. He lied, of course. He said he followed Drebber for a ways and then Drebber took a cab and he left off following him. Soon after, he met an old shipmate and walked a while with him. He couldn't tell me where I could find this shipmate, however.

"I think it went rather well," he continued, "and when I think of Lestrade riding off in the wrong direction it makes me —"

The door flew open and there stood Lestrade. Unlike Gregson's manner, his was troubled. He appeared to have come to seek advice from Holmes and was nonplussed to see Gregson there.

Watson wondered if this attitude was part of a ruse, or whether Lestrade's discomfort was genuine. He wished someone could manage to slip him information about what was going on. In the meantime, he could only act his part as he understood it.

"This is the most extraordinary case," Lestrade said at last. "Most incomprehensible."

"Ah, you find it so my friend," said Gregson triumphantly. "Have you managed to land the secretary, Stangerson?"

"Yes, I have. He was murdered at Halliday's Private Hotel at about six o'clock this morning."

Watson was stunned by this news and believed Holmes was also. Gregson acted surprised also. Watson knew the police were looking for Stangerson to inform him of his employer's death, but for Stangerson to be murdered was an unaccountable coincidence. Holmes was concentrating on Lestrade's report, so Watson glanced at Gregson and got a wink in return. So Gregson knew about Stangerson's "murder." Watson was baffled.

"Stangerson, too," Holmes mused. "The plot thickens."

"Are you sure, Lestrade?" asked a seemingly puzzled Inspector Gregson.

"I have just come from his room. I was the one who discovered the body."

"Is everything left undisturbed in the room?"

Holmes asked.

"Certainly. I thought you would want to view it yourself. I know that's what you prefer."

"Then, gentlemen, let's be off." Saying this, Holmes fetched his hat and coat and led the way down the stairs and on to the street. The others tried with difficulty to keep up.

Lestrade had had the hansom, in which he'd come, wait for him. He and Holmes entered it and started off. Gregson hailed another approaching hansom. Watson urgently began asking questions of Gregson even as they were mounting to their seats.

"For heavens sake man tell me what's going on."

"Oh, it's running beautifully, sir. Lestrade and I are having the time of our lives. We may just give up the Yard for a life on stage." He sensed Watson's impatience and went on, "Well sir, first of all, we learned that one reporter had ferreted out the address of the boarding house where Drebber had been staying. Dr. Neal became afraid Sherlock Holmes might—'extend' is the word he used—might extend his delusion to include the people at Charpentier's boarding house. So, we concocted the fiction I just related to you, so Mr. Holmes, who already thinks so little of our abilities, would dismiss my brilliant detective work and along with it any further thoughts concerning the Charpentiers.

"Just at the moment that I was about to set out for your lodgings with this yarn, we heard from Lestrade, who had been looking for Stangerson, as you know, to tell him about his employer's death. Lestrade reasoned that the two men might well have had an agreement to meet at a specific place should they become separated. As we knew, Drebber had at the last minute decided to look at the Lauriston Gardens property before he left London. To Lestrade, a hotel near Euston Station seemed a likely rendezvous. He tried several in the vicinity during the night without success and was about to give it up as a bad job and break off his search and go home, when he came by Halliday's Private Hotel. A constable approached him and repored that a man had just been observed climbing down a ladder that was leaning against the rear wall of the building. The man got away but the description given by a boy delivering milk in the alley was exactly that of John Salt, a burglar well known to the police of that neighborhood.

"Lestrade decided to check the hotel's registration book since he was there and he discovered Stangerson's name. When he went up to the second floor room, he noticed a ribbon of blood running out into the hall from under the door. He immediately got the night clerk to open the door. They found Stangerson stabbed to death, killed in an apparent struggle with the intruder. By this time the constables had apprehended Johnny Salt at a nearby grog shop. They discovered five gold sovereigns on his person. He claimed they were payment for a loan he'd made, but couldn't remember the debtor's name. He also claimed to have been in the grog shop for an hour but the tapster gave the constables a wink and a nod. They arrested Salt for Stangerson's murder."

Watson and Gregson's cab was following close upon that of Lestrade and Holmes, which was now passing Great Portland Street where Marylebone Road becomes Euston Street. Watson was wondering how Holmes was going to fit Stangerson's murder into his delusional theory about Mormons. He was also concerned that this real murder would seriously complicate their therapeutic plans for Holmes. He was puzzled why Gregson seemed so sanguine.

"I'm confused, Inspector. Why isn't the news about this murder being kept from Holmes? Why on earth are we going to the scene of the crime?"

"Ah, you see, sir, the three of us put our heads together and concluded that in Stangerson's murder we had another situation similar to Drebber's death. We were able to allow Mr. Holmes to investigate the 'murder' of Drebber, because there was in fact no unsolved murder. In Stangerson's case, we already had the killer behind bars. We could, therefore, afford to alter the scene in his hotel room to support Mr. Holmes' theories. Once that was done we would bring Mr. Holmes to the hotel and let him 'investigate' once again."

"Incredible! And what exact alterations did you make in the room?" Watson queried.

"You'll see soon enough. If I don't tell, you can better react with true surprise." With this Gregson gave a short snort of laughter and fell silent.

Watson saw that Gregson doubted his skill as an actor. Oh, the snobbery of the tyro. At the same time, Watson looked upon his companion with a newfound respect. Knowing all along about Stangerson's death and of the dressing-up of the crime scene, he had been able to come to Baker Street and give that perfect comic performance of the puffed-up, bumbling detective who had "arrested" young Arthur Charpentier, a performance that had without doubt taken in Sherlock Holmes.

The lead cab pulled over to the curb in front of Halliday's Private Hotel, and Holmes and Inspector Lestrade were already alighting, as the second hansom came to a halt behind it. The constable posted at the hotel's entrance saluted Lestrade, who led the way into the building and up the stairs to Stangerson's room. Sherlock Holmes was eagerly following. In the hallway outside the door Lestrade stopped and pointed to a puddle of blood on the floor.

Holmes stepped forward to take hold of the door handle. "If you gentlemen will permit me, I would like to enter the room alone and get a first impression using my full concentration. First, let me be sure about one thing. You're certain, Lestrade, that nothing has been altered in the room?"

Here was an unexpected direct challenge not anticipated by any of the conspirators. It not only required Lestrade to lie about the condition of the crime scene, it also put Lestrade's status as an honest professional at stake.

"Well, uh I . . . that is . . . " he began.

"I see," sneered Holmes, "untouched as far as you know. But, what your minions do when undirected is still something that remains undisciplined in the force." Under Holmes' breath, Watson could make out, "Such is reality."

"Oh, there is this," Lestrade hurried to say, while holding out a telegram. "It was in a book on the night stand."

"Thank you, Inspector," Holmes said, enunciating

131

each word separately and with dramatic irony. He opened the telegram, read it and handed it back to Lestrade.

"It tells me nothing I didn't already know," he commented dismissively.

The gaslight near the door was burning. Holmes, looking into the room said, "Did you light the lamp, Inspector?"

"Yes. I had the night clerk light it when we first entered the room; it was just at dawn."

"Just so."

From the open doorway the three men watched as Sherlock Holmes made his way around the room, pausing to gaze intently at different details.

The detail that Watson noticed first, aside from Stangerson's body sprawled upon the floor, was the word "Rache" written on the wall in what was no doubt Stangerson's blood. Although Holmes must certainly have seen it as well, he seemed to purposely avoid acknowledging it.

He became, instead, intensely interested in the night stand next to the bed, where he picked up and studied the open edge of an envelope. At this point he reached into his coat pocket and was heard to utter a disgusted self-reproach, "My glass, damn my carelessness!" Following this he turned his attention to Stangerson's corpse, which lay on its side. The pool of blood extended from the chest out toward the open doorway, where the others stood looking on. Holmes pushed the upper part of the torso back so he could view the bloody front of the man's shirt.

"You have observed that this man was stabbed with his own knife, I presume."

"No. Do you think so?" Lestrade answered with surprise.

"Yes, of course. But then . . . It must be." He stood and began scanning the room. "Ah yes, what have we here?" he said with triumph as he strode over to the window where Watson could see him pick up a small, white, wooden box off the windowsill. He opened it, sniffed the contents and walked over to the doorway where he showed the box's contents to his small audience. The box contained two small, round, pearl-gray pills.

"The last link, gentlemen. My case is now complete."

He walked out into the hall taking care not to step in the blood.

"But what about the writing on the wall?" pursued Watson, incredulous that Holmes seemed to be ignoring the gory message.

"Oh that. Yes, the same hand wrote it, but it has

little importance. Shall we go back to Baker Street? I shall conduct a demonstration, which should prove to be very convincing to one and all."

On the ride back to Baker Street, Gregson obliged Watson with a complete account of the alterations which he, Lestrade, and I had made to the crime scene.

"When Lestrade found the body, the drawers of the chest were all pulled out. Johnny Salt had clearly been searching through them for valuables when Stangerson awoke and discovered him. Stangerson's sturdy letter-opener must have been lying on the nightstand. He grabbed this up and attacked Salt, but in the struggle the knife was driven into Stangerson's own heart. By the way, Johnny Salt had never been known to carry a weapon or to have ever assaulted anyone. It would only be in a life-and-death struggle for the knife that he would have killed the man. As Mr. Holmes said, the letter-opener belonged to Stangerson; it has his initials on it, but I'll be a monkey's uncle if I can figure out how Holmes knew the letter-opener had been used rather than a knife that the murderer had brought with him."

"So you have the letter-opener?"

"Yes, yes, of course, it was in Stangerson's heart. We removed it because we reasoned that if this Jefferson Hope had come to kill Stangerson in revenge, he would have come with a good knife for the purpose. Holmes would never believe he would have relied upon using the man's own letter-opener as a weapon to force him to swallow the poison."

"Poison?" a confused Watson said. "Oh yes, the pills in the box. So, you wanted Sherlock to believe Jefferson Hope used his own knife—but, instead, Holmes deduced correctly Stangerson's own knife was the murder weapon."

"Exactly. I'm hoping our not leaving a knife doesn't give our game away. Too much goes on in that mind of his."

They rode in silence for a few minutes before Watson spoke. "I assume you wrote, 'Rache.'"

"Yes. Dr. Neal wrote it as he did the first time."

"And the pill box?"

"Right. Because Mr. Holmes said Drebber was poisoned, Dr. Neal thought we should stick to the same modus operandi. The pills are not poison, of course. We couldn't take a chance on anything like that. Dr. Neal went to a chemist's shop and had the chemist make up two pills of a water-soluble, inert substance used in the compounding of medications. Dr. Neal also obtained a tin of the same silver polish he had used to daub Drebber's lips. He touched the inside of a pillbox with enough of the polish to give it the same odor that Holmes had smelled on Drebber's lips."

Gregson continued to review in his mind the changes that the three of them had made to the crime scene.

"Almost forgot: The other thing we did was to close the drawers of the chest to hide the fact that a burglary was in progress. I guess that's all we did."

"What about the telegram that Lestrade said was found in a book on the night stand? What was in it?"

"Oh yes, forgot my own handiwork," replied Gregson smiling broadly. "That was my own idea and not a bad one if I do say so. The telegram which Lestrade had sent to Mr. Holmes from the telegraph office, after you alerted Dr. Neal about the telegram to Cleveland, mentioned that Jefferson Hope had left America for Europe. I thought it would add a bit of icing to the cake if I got the same telegraph agent to make us up another telegram with the message, 'J.H. is in Europe.' It was dated a week ago and it was unsigned. I wanted it to look like somebody, acting as a lookout for these two fugitives from the avenging Jefferson Hope, had warned them of his pursuit.

"Lestrade took care of that while I was on my way to tell you about my 'arrest' of Arthur Charpentier."

"Icing indeed!" Watson exclaimed. "Very clever, Inspector, and Sherlock Holmes certainly accepted it as authentic. He took it as confirmation of what he 'already knew'. Interesting how gullible we can become when something compliments our own point of view."

"So far so good," concluded Gregson.

Watson slapped the detective on the knee. "Remember, old man, that's what the chap said as he fell out of the belfry."

Gregson laughed heartily and then suddenly stopped. "What do you suppose this demonstration is that Mr. Holmes was talking about?"

"Your guess is as good as mine, Inspector."

By the time Watson and Gregson's cab completed the return journey to Baker Street, the cab, which bore Holmes and Lestrade there, had already rejoined the dense morning traffic. Watson entered the front vestibule to see Holmes standing next to their tearful landlady. At their feet on a pillow rested the landlady's ailing old terrier.

"Watson, would you mind carrying the poor little devil up to our rooms?" Although qualified by the phrase "would you mind," Watson heard more of an instruction than a request.

The old dog whimpered when he picked it and the cushion up, but then it nuzzled its snowy head against his chest as he followed Holmes up the stairs and into their apartment where he laid the cushion and dog down on the carpet in the sitting room.

The two inspectors had just entered the sitting room, when Holmes withdrew the pillbox taken from Stangerson's hotel room from his pocket. He opened the box and held it out toward Watson.

"Doctor, would you say these are ordinary pills?"

Watson took the box from Holmes and feigned to study the two small, round, translucent balls in the box. Of course Gregson had already told him of their composition. He wondered how much he could safely say.

"I would say from their appearance that they are water-soluble." He was about to go perhaps too far and add something about the odor, when Holmes cut him off.

"Precisely so. I will now cut one of them in half," he said, taking out his penknife. He did so and returned one half of the pill to the box. He walked over to a table where a silver tray held four wine glasses and two crystal decanters, one of sherry, the other of water. "This half pill I will put in this glass, to which I add a teaspoonful of water." He held up the glass. "You will perceive that the

138

good doctor is right. It readily dissolves."

The three conspirators were beginning to be worried. They had hoped the odor of the pills alone would satisfy Sherlock Holmes that they were the same "poison" which had killed Enoch Drebber.

Lestrade ventured, "What has their being soluble in water got to do with the death of Mr. Joseph Stangerson, since there is no doubt that he was stabbed to death?"

"Patience, my friend, patience! You will find it has everything to do with it. Now I shall add a little milk to make the mixture palatable and pour it onto this saucer."

Holmes then looked each man in the eyes and explained, "The landlady asked me yesterday if I couldn't do something to put her dog, which has been ill so long, out of its misery. My little demonstration gives me the opportunity to answer her request."

He knelt beside the poor old dog and offered him the saucer. The dog lapped it up.

The others watched this demonstration with a mixture of anxiety and horror, anxiety that Holmes was about to find out that the pills were harmless and horror that he intended to poison the poor old dog right there in front of them in order to prove a point. The dog, meanwhile, settled again on the pillow in apparent comfort.

Holmes sat down and took out his watch, checking it as minute followed minute with no result. He gnawed his lip, drummed his fingers on the table. His displeasure and agitation grew.

"It can't be a coincidence," he cried, springing out of his chair and pacing about the room. "It is impossible that it should be mere coincidence. The very pills which I suspected in the case of Drebber are actually found after Stangerson's murder, and yet they are inert. What can it mean? Surely my whole chain of reasoning cannot have been false."

The others, observing Holmes's pain of self-doubt, realized that their great plan was about to collapse if Holmes were forced by reason to abandon his theory. Watson feared the delusion of being "the world's greatest detective" would evaporate only to be replaced by a more pernicious and expansively paranoid one.

"It is impossible," Holmes repeated, "And yet this wretched dog is none the worse. Aha! . . . I have it!" With a shriek of delight, he withdrew the box from his pocket and cut the remaining pill in half and dissolved it in a little water to which he again added milk. This he transferred to the saucer and offered to the terrier. The dog had barely finished drinking it, when it gave a shiver in every limb, then lay lifeless.

Sherlock Holmes drew a long breath of relief and took a handkerchief from his pocket and wiped his forehead. "I should have more faith. I ought to know by this time that when a fact appears to be opposed to a long train of deductions it invariably proves to be capable of bearing some other interpretation. Of the two pills in that box, one was of the most deadly poison, and the other was entirely harmless. I ought to have known that before I ever saw the box."

The three other men stared at the lifeless creature lying on the carpet in mouth-gaping amazement. How could it be that one of the pills was truly poisonous?

Holmes misinterpreted their reaction and felt what was for him an unusual degree of sympathy with their confusion.

"I quite understand. All this seems strange to you, because you failed at the beginning of the inquiry to grasp the importance of the single real clue that was presented to you. I had the good fortune to seize upon it, and everything that has occurred since then has served to confirm my original supposition. Indeed, everything that occurred has been the logical sequence of it. Hence, the things that have perplexed you and made the case more obscure have served to enlighten me and to strengthen my conclusions. It is a mistake to confound strangeness with mystery. The most commonplace crime is frequently the most mysterious, because it presents no new or special features from which deductions may be drawn."

Watson intuited that Gregson believed their caper had reached its intended goal. Sherlock Holmes had, in his own mind, securely enthroned himself as the world's greatest and first consulting detective. The present game needed to be brought to a conclusion. He and Lestrade both had much work to attend to which had been piling up while they had been occupied with this . . . whim. It had been a bit of a lark in its way, but it was time to get back to real work. Besides, he and Lestrade had absorbed as much of Holmes's derision as they cared to. Gregson caught Watson's eye, conveyed his feelings with a look, and received a nod of approval.

Gregson used the frontal approach - the one in harmony with his own personality. "Look here, Mr. Holmes, we're all ready to acknowledge that you are a smart man, and that you have your own methods of working. It seems I was wrong in arresting young Charpentier. You have thrown out hints here and there, and seem to know more than we do, but the time has come when we feel we have a right to ask you straight out: Can you name the man who did it?"

John Watson put his oar in the water. "Any delay

in arresting the assassin might give him time to commit some fresh atrocity."

Watson, Lestrade and Gregson expected Sherlock Holmes to name the young, revenge-seeking lover of Holmes's Mormon fantasy, Jefferson Hope. And since Jefferson Hope could never be apprehended, being but an apparition, his name must now harmlessly join the many files of wanted men.

Holmes began walking about the room, his head sunk on his chest, obviously deep in thought. He stopped and faced the others. "There will be no new murders. You can forget that possibility. Can I name the man? Yes I can, but that is a small thing compared to laying our hands on him. This I expect to do very shortly. It needs delicate handling, however. This is a shrewd and dangerous man and he has the support of another who is as clever as he. As long as he has no clue that we suspect him, there is a chance of catching him, but if he has the slightest suspicion he will change his name and vanish in an instant into the four million inhabitants of this great city."

"Egads," thought Watson. "It's like having a tiger by the tail. There's no way to let it go."

Sherlock Holmes directed his attention to the two inspectors. "Without meaning to hurt either of your feelings, I am bound to say that these men are more than a match for the official force, and that is why I have not asked for your assistance. If I fail I shall, of course, incur all the blame for this omission, but that I am prepared for."

This latest slur against the police was almost more than either inspector could swallow. Gregson was red to the roots of his flaxen hair and Lestrade's eyes glistened with resentment. But before either had a chance to slip and give vent to their feelings, there was a tap at the sitting room door.

Wiggins, the spokesman for Holmes's squad of street-orphans, entered the room, ragged cap in hand, saw that he was confronted with two policemen whom he immediately recognized and froze.

"What is it, Wiggins? Have you found him?"

"Yes, sir. The cab is downstairs."

"Excellent!" Holmes had trouble hiding his elation. "The cabman might as well help me with my luggage, Wiggins. Ask him to come up."

Holmes hurried to his room and returned with a portmanteau, which he laid on the floor. In his hand he also held a pair of handcuffs that he dropped into his pocket. He busied himself with the strap of the suitcase.

Right then a man entered the room whom both Lestrade and Gregson recognized, having met him two days earlier at number 3 Lauriston Gardens.

"Just give me a hand with this buckle," said Holmes, looking up and addressing the newcomer.

The man hesitated a moment, wondering why he was being appealed to, but then went over and obligingly bent down to assist Sherlock Holmes.

In an instant, there was a sound of clicking metal and Sherlock Holmes sprang back.

"Gentlemen, let me introduce the murderer of Enoch Drebber and Joseph Stangerson."

Lestrade and Gregson were completely taken aback since they knew the handcuffed man as James Brock, the estate agent who had been with Enoch Drebber when he suffered a heart attack and died. Lestrade got as far as saying, "See here," when the handcuffed man issued a cry of rage and launched himself toward the window. All four men lunged to prevent him from crashing through, and only after using all their combined strength did they manage to subdue him and force him to the floor.

At the height of this struggle another man, dressed like a cab driver, came to the open door of the sitting room and observing the violence retreated quickly, unnoticed by the others, back down the stairs.

The manacled man finally gave up struggling, completely relaxed and sighed in abject resignation, "All right, you've got me."

Leaving the man to the two inspectors, Holmes rose and said triumphantly, "We have reached the end of our little mystery. You can use his cab, which is waiting below, to take him to the police station, and when you return from there, you are very welcome to put any question you like to me. There is no longer reason to fear that I will refuse to answer."

A handcuffed James Brock, whom Holmes thought to be Jefferson Hope, was hustled out of the apartment, an inspector each holding an arm. Watson got his coat from the chair where he had thrown it earlier and, putting it on, began to follow.

"Here, Watson there is no need for you to go. Our bit in all this has come to an end," said Holmes.

John Watson hesitated. He thought he detected a tinge of fear in his companion's voice and wondered at it. It added to an impression he had already begun to form that Sherlock Holmes, while deeply invested in fantasies of crime was, in fact, in dread of actual violence and anything to do with the reality of punishment, including the interior of a police station. Watson intuited Sherlock's fear that the two detectives would witness his anxiety and recognize this underlying fear, a fear not very becoming in the "world's greatest detective." If Watson's intuition was sound, then he should comply with Holmes's instructions to remain with him in their apartment. But he also wanted to leave with the police so he could send word to me, Brandon Neal, to go straightaway to the police station. Besides, he also wanted to learn what this man's "confession" was all about. He was forced to think quickly and the reply that he hit upon would commit him to a labor that would forever alter the world of crime literature.

"But I must go, Holmes. You see I have decided to use my journal notes to write a book about this case and your unique methods. I am determined that the world must know."

Holmes couldn't hide the pleasure he experienced from John Watson's announcement, but tried to appear disinterested. "A waste of time in my opinion, because my methods are way ahead of their time and your book will suffer the same fate as all precocious insights. But, if you must, I suppose you must."

Holmes turned to fill his pipe from the Persian slipper where his tobacco was kept, but not before Watson caught a glimpse in Holmes of what he could only call euphoria.

Recognizing how powerful a published

account would be in furthering our treatment project to fortify the delusion of "World's greatest and first consulting detective," John Watson did write the b o o k . He called it *A Study in Scarlet,* publishing it first in serialized form in *Strand Magazine* under a pen name that was a compilation of the first names of Watson's three uncles. In 1888 Ward Locke & Co. brought out the hard cover edition.

Watson and I both realized that while Holmes's knowledge of the public's new awareness of his "powers" would strengthen his identity as the great detective, this notoriety would also inflate his towering narcissism. We had, however, no notion of the popularity that Watson's doctored accounts of Sherlock's "cases" would enjoy. It was chiefly because of that popularity that I have been unable to publish the account of Sherlock Holmes's treatment.

The format was simple: in each and every scene in which Sherlock Holmes was a participant, *A Study in Scarlet* presented the action and dialogue verbatim. After all, since Holmes had act u ally been present, he would have quickly identified any fabrication by Watson. Not included, of course, were the machinations of our treatment plan, such as setting the stage for each of the two "murders."

Fabrication of Holmes's participation only occurred in the material I am now about to relate. That was necessary to spare Holmes the embarrassment of having his phobias of violence and prisons revealed to the reading public. So in the book Watson has Holmes accompany the two detectives and himself to the police station to hear Jefferson Hope's confession. It was apparently a fabrication welcomed by Holmes, because he never afterward complained to Watson of this inaccuracy.   B.N.

Watson hurried after the two detectives and their prisoner and joined them as they came onto the street. Two four-wheel cabs were waiting at the kerb, each with a driver. Watson was surprised for a moment, since the driver of the one cab was supposedly in handcuffs. Lestrade and Gregson commandeered the nearest cab to transport their prisoner. They both climbed in with the man between them and started off toward the station.

Watson approached the second cab.

"Will you be Mr. Holmes? The driver asked.

"No," Watson answered, puzzled by the man's question.

Watson told the driver to wait and hurried to

the tobacconist shop on the corner and gave the assistant a message to be delivered immediately to me, Brandon Neal, alerting me to the state of things. Having done this, he returned to the waiting cab and told the driver to make his way as fast as p o s sible to the police station. All the way there Watson puzzled over the strange and unexpected occurrence he had just been party to. Who could this man be who seemingly admitted his guilt for killing Drebber and Stangerson? He couldn't be Jefferson Hope as Holmes seemed to imply. Or could he? If that were true then Watson's world had just turned upside-down. Another detail in particular nagged him. The street urchin named Wiggins had come upstairs and announced that a cab driver was outside, and Holmes told Wiggins to have the cabbie come up and help him with his luggage, yet the man who presented himself moments later was clearly not a cabman.

Watson's cab made good time weaving in and out of the traffic and arrived at the police station just as the inspectors and their charge were alighting from the other vehicle. Watson got down, paid his driver and began to follow the others into the building when a thought, seemingly from nowhere, caused him to turn back and cry out to his driver.

"I say Cabbie, wait a moment," he called out.

The man reined in his horse and looked down. "Yes gov'nor, what is it?"

"I have a question."

"Yes?"

"What is your name, my good fellow?"

Instantly the cabman became wary. The question of why this bloke wanted to know his name was written on his face.

Watson saw his mistake and added, "You see, I was wondering if your name, by chance, is Jefferson Hope?"

"And what if it is? And *what*, I'd like to know, is all this interest in my name? The young tyke asked me my name and then said a Mr. Holmes wanted to hire my cab at 221B Baker Street."

"Well I'll be," murmured Watson, his hand going to his chin. He looked up again at the driver. "I don't suppose you've ever been to America."

"America? What is this, some kind of joke? I tell you it's an evil sense of humor that makes light of a man trying to earn bread for his family's table."

"I assure you there was no joke or harm intended. It's just a case of mistaken identity."

Watson reached into his pocket and took out a half-crown. "For your trouble, my good man."

Watson stood staring after the cab as it pulled

away from the kerb. First the death of the dog and now this amazing coincidence—there really was in London a cab driver named Jefferson Hope. But Watson had long realized that coincidence, most of it unrecognized, shapes our daily lives. He shrugged and entered the police station.

Both inspectors were thoroughly confused by Brock's confession to a crime. They were puzzled by his attempt at flight followed by his resigned cry of, "All right, you've got me." But out of deeply ingrained experience they were inclined to hold on to anyone who confessed a crime until they knew the facts. Some time passed before they could arrange for a room where an uninterrupted interrogation of Brock was possible.

I abruptly canceled my scheduled appointments as soon as I received Watson's message. The time that elapsed before the prisoner could be interviewed, allowed me to rush to the police station to make up a fourth member of the interrogating team that faced Mr. James Brock.

While completely confused by Brock's confession, but neither inspector let on that they had any doubt about it.

Lestrade began the interview. "Your story will be taken down by Inspector Gregson and you will be asked to read it and sign it afterward. Now then, tell us everything that happened."

Brock was a thoroughly beaten man. His tale was related with a sad finality, as of a man who had known many failures and was now acknowledging the final, fatal event of his life. His voice was saturated with defeat.

"It started out just as I told you when I reported Mr. Drebber's death. He came to my office and inquired about an inexpensive house he could buy. He said he was an antiques dealer from Cleveland and came yearly to England to buy and send antiques back to his store in America. He wanted a place where he could store the articles he bought and at the same time have a place where he and his assistant could stay when they were in this country searching out antiques. The idea was economy. I had the listing of the property in Lauriston Gardens to let, but I was sure the owner would be glad of the opportunity to sell it. It had stood empty for some time, you see. Like a glove does a hand, the house fit Mr. Drebber's needs. I very much needed the commission from such a sale. My business is failing and I am sorely worried about the future for my wife and two children. Mr. Drebber said he was able to pay cash for the purchase. Because he and his assistant were returning to America, he wanted to complete the transaction that day if the building suited him. They had wanted to catch the Liverpool Express that day, but he had decided to delay their travel until the next day after he'd heard my assurance that the Lauriston Gardens house was ideal for him and at a very good price. Mr. Drebber said he needed to go to meet his assistant to tell him of the decision to view the house and would return to my office soon and go with me to view the property. I was worried that he was only saying this to have an excuse to leave, and I would not see him again. But, he was as good as his word and was back within the hour.

"We came straightway to the house in a cab. It was dark when we got there and all I had for light was a candle that I lit in the downstairs rooms. Drebber stood there and listened while I walked about describing the improvements that could be made without undue expense. I was excited by the prospect of the sale and what happened next has not been an uncommon occurrence when I am overly excited—my nose began to bleed. The blood flowed freely. Suddenly, I heard him fall. I thought the sight of all the blood had caused him to faint. Then I noticed he was lying very still indeed. He had, in fact, stopped breathing. I was beside myself. Could he have had a stroke and died? Of all the things that could have happened to me, this seemed the worst. I walked about, still bleeding, wondering what to do.

"It was my desperate financial situation that

determined the direction of my thinking. It occurred to me that Drebber had said he was able to pay cash that day, so it was likely he would have the money on him. I searched him but found none. I calmed down a bit and realized it would cause me no real trouble to notify the police and tell the truth—except about searching Drebber's body."

James Brock paused and seeing that Gregson was still writing furiously to catch up with the story, waited. When he did resume he did so in the dismal voice of a condemned man.

"It was only when I was telling the story to the constable that it occurred to me that if Drebber didn't have the cash then his assistant, Joseph Stangerson, must have it. When Drebber had returned to my office after excusing himself to meet his assistant, he mentioned off hand that the assistant's name was Stangerson and they would be spending the night at Halliday's Private Hotel near Euston Station. On impulse I withheld that information from the constable. I couldn't b e l i e v e what my mind was contemplating. I have always been law-abiding, yet here I was entertaining the idea of breaking into Mr. Stangerson's room and stealing the money. It seemed the only thing I could do for my family because you see, gentlemen, I have a serious heart disease from which I might die at any moment—

die and leave my family with no means of support."

"What kind of a problem?" Lestrade demanded.

"I don't know what it's called, but the doctor only had to feel my chest and tell me the truth."

Dr. Watson got up and went over to Brock and felt inside the man's jacket, then, with a startled tone he exclaimed, "An aneurysm! The man is telling the truth."

The men looked at James Brock with a mixture of alarm, pity and suspended judgment in anticipation of the completion of his story. To this end Gregson made a gesture to indicate he was ready to resume writing down Brock's statement.

"The death of Mr. Drebber was reported in the morning papers," continued Brock, "but I thought it likely Stangerson, being a foreigner, would not read the newspaper of a strange city, and therefore would not know of his employer's death. In other words, I thought it was very likely I could still find him at Halliday's Private Hotel.

"Yesterday I scouted out the lay of the land around the hotel and, without raising suspicion, I was able to discover not only that Mr. Stangerson was still registered, but also which room he occupied. I also spotted a ladder conveniently lying alongside a neighboring building where some work was being done. I returned just before dawn this morning. At that hour

I figured I had the greatest chance to find him deeply asleep. I leaned the ladder against the hotel wall and climbed to Stangerson's window. It opened easily and I was able to climb into the room without any noise. First, I satisfied myself that the man was sound asleep and then I went to the door where his jacket hung and searched the pockets, finding them empty. Next I went to the chest-of-drawers and began going through them. It was then I heard a noise behind me and turned just in time to ward off Stangerson, who was coming at me with a knife. My quick reaction threw him off balance and enabled me to grab for the hand holding the knife. I got a firm grip while at the same time he twisted around attempting to get out of my grasp. I didn't feel anything different, but it must have been then that the knife entered his chest. He gave a cry and fell to the floor with me on top of him. That must have driven the blade home. He made no further movement or sound. The man was dead.

"I quickly climbed back down the ladder. As I reached the bottom, I noticed a boy entering the alley delivering milk. I sank down behind a dustbin just as another man came down the alley. I think he had been drinking for he looked neither right nor left, but kept his eyes straight ahead on his staggering course. When both he and the boy were gone, I made my way home."

Gregson caught up with his writing and looked up, waiting for Brock to continue.

"That's all there is to the story," Brock said, totally depleted. "I went round to the Lauriston Gardens house later this morning to be sure it was locked up properly and while there I found this magnifying glass on the mantle next to a spot where blood had been smeared on the wall." Brock took a large glass from his pocket, one that Watson and the two inspectors had seen before in the hands of Sherlock Holmes. "The bloody writing surprised me, for I knew not how it came to be there. At this time, you understand, I was feeling very frightened that it would be discovered that I was the one in Mr. Stangerson's room. I thought it would look good for me to be the good citizen returning the magnifying glass to its owner who, after all, could only be among the police who had investigated Mr. Drebber's death. I found and asked the constable to whom I had first reported the death. He told me that he had seen such a glass being employed by a Mr. Sherlock Holmes and I learned his address. I came up to his room for the purpose of returning it to him when I was surprised, as you gentlemen know, by that gentleman asking me to help him secure a strap on his luggage."

Tears appeared in Brock's eyes. His despair was deep.

"When I felt those manacles on my wrist, I knew all was lost. In some way—the way you detectives have—I had been found out."

A silence fell on the scene. Watson and Lestrade and I watched as Gregson reversed the document he had penned and handed the pen to James Brock who, without reading it, signed it.

I thought about the fate of poor John Salt if Brock hadn't made his confession. He might well have swung on the gallows for the murder of Stangerson.

The prisoner was led away leaving us four conspirators together. The silence, which had begun with the end of Brock's confession, continued until Gregson broke down laughing. Astonished, we three looked on as Gregson reached the point where he was having trouble breathing.

"What on earth is so funny?" scolded Lestrade.

Struggling to get control, Gregson gasped out, "Don't you see? In the end Sherlock Holmes got his man."

The meaning sank in and soon all four of us were laughing out of control.

Such laughter can only be sustained for so long and at its end, it was I who spoke, summing up what all felt.

"Gentlemen, it has been an unpredictable and wild ride. I find it hard to believe, but we accomplished what we set out to do. Mycroft Holmes has reported to me that there has been no bizarre spying around the Ministry during the past days. It is also his opinion that his brother hasn't been using drugs recently. What about that, John?"

"Definitely. Aside from the basic delusion, which we set out to enhance, I have seen no spreading of his paranoid ideas beyond the Mormon menace which, as you all know, he thinks he has just conquered. But our work is not yet finished. Don't forget Holmes expects us to return to Baker Street to hear his explanation of how he 'solved' the problem. I think you all agree with me that giving him the chance to lecture us is a necessary part of the whole treatment."

"Ah yes," I agreed "But I fortunately must be excluded from that lecture."

I was moved by the fact that John Watson's main interest was in the welfare and treatment of his patient.

"Lucky stiff," Lestrade said to me and then looked at his colleague. "Tobias, at least both of us need not attend. One of us can have the excuse that he must attend to the paperwork on the prisoner. What say we flip a coin?"

"Fair enough." Gregson took a coin from his pocket and tossed it in the air.

"Heads," called out Lestrade. And heads it was.

"Shite!" Gregson cried.

We others laughed at him and he too began to smile and said, "All in the line of duty, I suppose."

Watson and Gregson left us, preparing themselves for the lecture that awaited them at Baker Street.

"Inspector," I said to Lestrade, "I hope the paperwork you spoke of can wait, because I need your assistance on another matter. Mycroft Holmes and I realized that when the case came to a conclusion, Homes would be very likely to look to the newspaper for an account of it. We concluded that it was critical for him to find there a report that confirms the facts as we have caused him to experience them. Otherwise, his sharp intelligence would quickly detect something fishy.

"I have with me a letter from the Home Secretary directing the Managing Editor of *The Echo*, Sherlock's favorite newspaper, to cooperate fully with the police in creating a page to be inserted in a single copy of the paper, the copy which will be delivered to 221B Baker Street tomorrow morning. We have little time to lose if the newspaper is to be able to accomplish this."

"A special page?" Lestrade wondered.

"Yes, we will make it up in the cab on the way to the newspaper office."

So two cabs were hailed to go to our separate tasks. Watson yelled after me as his cab departed.

"Give all the credit to the police and none to Sherlock. He's sure to believe it's authentic in that case."

"Right on, John. A very good idea."

At that moment a constable ran out of the building, calling to Lestrade.

"Sir, wait a moment!"

He ran up to us out of breath. "The prisoner, sir. On the way to the cell, he fell down . . . He's dead, sir."

The Editor of *The Echo* was not best pleased with the request Inspector Lestrade made. Indeed, if it had only had the authority of a request from a Scotland Yard inspector it might well have been rejected. The wording of the letter from the Home Secretary left little doubt, however, that it was a request which couldn't be refused. That is, not if the paper banked on the goodwill and cooperation of the government for much of the information it needed.

"Just what is the text that you want on this special page?" the editor asked in an even voice that acquiesced while attempting to preserve dignity.

I held out the two pages torn from my notebook on which Lestrade and I had composed our piece.

The editor gave it a newspaperman's appraisal.

"Half column. Twenty lines there about. And the

rest of the page is to be according to the regular edition?"

"As much as possible, yes," I answered.

"Very well. Tell the Home Secretary that we are very happy to be of service."

Tobias Gregson and John Watson made their way back to Baker Street. Settled into chairs in the sitting room, they were resigned to the task of sitting through Holmes's self-laudatory lecture. Gregson looked to Holmes and spoke clearly, still enjoying his thespian role.

"Mr. Holmes, we have heard Jefferson Hope's confession, but before I tell you any details of what the man said to us, I'm taking you up on your pledge to explain your method and the steps followed in your deduction. I have come to hear this and carry it back to Inspector Lestrade, who regrets he can't be here since he must attend to our prisoner."

Disappointment registered on Sherlock's face. The audience for the great revelation had been reduced by a third. Holmes recovered his poise, apparently resigned to play to the "house" he had at hand. He was standing in front of the two seated men, wearing his frock coat as if before a university class. He took two paces toward the window before wheeling around suddenly.

"The wedding ring, gentlemen, was the key." He

paused dramatically as if he had just said, "The play's the thing." "Of course its importance went unappreciated by everyone else, but I knew in an instant that the ring had been held in front of the victim's eyes before he was forced to make the fateful choice of which pill to swallow."

Gregson and Watson were as baffled as if they were listening to a lecture in Kantian philosophy.

Sherlock's native exhibitionism told him he had just lost his tiny audience. He doubled back to retrieve them.

"Both of you will recall that I was nonplused when the dog survived swallowing the pill I gave him. I knew that Drebber had been poisoned and a box containing two unusual pills was discovered in Stangerson's room. I reasoned that the pills must be of the same poison used to kill Drebber. They also had the same odor to the one on Drebber's lips—that is, one of them did. If I had sniffed each pill separately, I would have immediately realized Jefferson Hope's method. You see, although it was obvious that Drebber had been poisoned, there remained a nagging problem that troubled me until the answer was revealed when the dog died. You both must see this."

Both men dearly wished they were able to speak up, but neither had a clue to what Holmes was talking about.

"Yes gentlemen, the question was, how did the murderer force Drebber to take a poisonous pill, especially in the absence of any sign of there having been a struggle? It was while puzzling over the fact that the dog didn't die when given the first pill that it all became as clear as day to me. Jefferson Hope was certainly a man bent on revenge for a grave injustice, yet he was committed to a sense of fair play and justice when it came to exacting retribution. What he did is offer his victim the choice of two pills, one poisonous and the other harmless. He himself would take the pill which remained—a form of duel. Admirable! Yes, very fair, but of course, he must have possessed a weapon that made it clear that the alternative to accepting the offered challenge would be sudden violent death. Mr. Enoch Drebber chose the wrong pill. Jefferson Hope's excitement must have been very high at that moment when he didn't know whether it would be Drebber or himself who would soon lie dead on the floor of that dreary room. That's what caused his nose to bleed. The sight of the blood, coupled with his exultation at surviving the duel while at the same time achieving the revenge he sought, suggested the triumphant declaration upon the wall, 'Rache.'

"As I just said, I didn't know this detail about the challenge until the poor mutt succumbed to the poison in the second pill. But aside from that, I knew the shape of the case. Only a few blanks remained to be filled in. The ring told me the revenge was about an affair of the heart. I suspected that Drebber had stolen the woman the murderer loved. I felt sure that the Cleveland police could supply the answer. This proved to be correct. Watson, you'll remember the telegram I sent after we had left the house at Lauriston Gardens. It was to Cleveland inquiring about Drebber's state of marriage. Their prompt reply confirmed that Drebber, now a widower, had already sought police protection from an old rival in love, Jefferson Hope, and this same man was now in Europe. The case was solved; there only remained the task of finding Jefferson Hope. I had reasoned from the footprints in the house and upon the path leading to it that only two men had entered the house. This I told you when we were at the house together. Now, I further noticed that the wheel marks in the road left by the cab they came in—a four-wheeled one—indicated that the horse had wandered some distance down the road. This could only have occurred if the horse was unattended for a while. Where could the driver have gone if not in the house?"

There was sufficient challenge in the tone with which this question was put forth that caused Watson to answer in his own mind, "He could have fallen asleep."

"That's right, gentlemen. The only place he could have been was in the house with Mr. Enoch Drebber. He had to be the second man whose square-toed shoes left so many prints in the dust on the floor. Therefore, I knew the murderer was a driver of a four-wheeled cab."

Sherlock opened his arms wide, palms up in the universal gesture meaning, "It's obvious!"

"I next employed my own Baker Street police force. I sent them forth to find a four wheel cab driver cabbie named, Jefferson Hope. The rest you witnessed. Young Wiggins reported to me here that they had succeeded and the man we sought was at the kerb with his vehicle. I told Wiggins to ask the man to come up and help me with my luggage. When he did so, I applied the handcuffs. He panicked, but soon realized there was no use to resist."

Sherlock Holmes smiled the benevolent smile of a parent who has just explained one of life's conundrums to a growing child.

"I know you both are thinking that it is all very simple, nothing very profound about my method or its results. It is the same when one is told how a magician manages one of his illusions. Simple when told, but baffling unless one is adept at the science of detection."

Watson's head snapped around to assess Gregson's reaction to this last mouthful. He saw a man fighting with an internal combustion. Gregson's face flushed, but he contained the emotion of outrage. In fact he managed a performance worthy of several curtain calls.

"Well, Mr. Holmes, I am truly in awe. It is too bad that the general public can't come to know and appreciate your genius. It so . . . "

"That omission may soon be remedied, my dear Gregson," said Holmes, beaming.

Gregson, not knowing Holmes was referring to Watson's stated intention of writing an account, was stalled for a moment and then thought of Stangerson's murder.

"If I follow your reasoning correctly, you believe Jefferson Hope surprised Drebber's assistant in his room and offered him the same choice of pills he had offered to Drebber the night before?"

"Very good, Gregson. That's exactly what happened."

"But why the assistant? I understood the grudge was between Drebber and Jefferson Hope."

"Don't you see that Stangerson was part of the original plot to force Lucy Ferrier into the despicable marriage?"

Holmes had become heated with impatience over Gregson's apparent density. Watson hastened to quench the flame.

"Yes, of course, that's obvious, but I have another question."

Holmes calmed down and addressed Watson in a tone that said there was at least one bright man in his audience.

"Yes, Doctor, what is on your mind?"

"At the hotel, you asked if we appreciated the fact that Stangerson was killed with his own knife. How did you arrive at that conclusion?"

"I was really addressing Inspector Lestrade then. I couldn't expect you and Gregson, who had not been in the room, to have noticed that the telegram envelope that lay on the bed stand had been opened with a very sharp knife. Since no knife was found in the room, the only explanation is that Stangerson had refused the duel proposed by Jefferson Hope and taken up the knife, quite possibly a sturdy letter-opener, and attacked Hope. In the ensuing struggle, it was Stangerson who was stabbed. Hope, no doubt wanting the police to believe the murderer was an intruder armed with a knife and bent upon robbery, carried the knife away with him."

Holmes was once more sanguine and Gregson seized the opportunity to escape.

"Well, sir, your account agreed in full with Jefferson Hope's confession. I know that Lestrade will be as impressed as I am." Getting up he added, "I am anxious to return to the station to relate all of this to him."

Holmes was surprised by Gregson's move and implored, "But surely you wish to hear the tale of monstrous tyranny that precipitated the sad spectacle that has been played out in our midst."

"How's that?"

"I mean the story of the Mormons of Utah and the young girl who came to be the object of lascivious tyranny."

Gregson looked to John Watson for guidance. He saw there a subtle signal that it was important that he settle back down in his chair to listen to Sherlock Holmes.

Thus Gregson was forced to pass one of the most boring hours of his life as Sherlock Holmes paced back and forth, spinning out the fantasy which had become a reality for him. His reluctant audience listened as he embellished with minute detail the story of a group of pioneers heading into the great American West, of starvation and death and of the survival of one little girl, Lucy, and an old trail guide. Holmes painted a sentimental picture of Lucy's innocent childhood among the Mormons who had come upon the starving child and had taken her along with them to Utah. He told of her falling in love with a handsome young stranger, Jefferson Hope (named after one of their nation's most illustrious presidents, Holmes explained), of their heart-rending separation while he journeyed to the gold fields of California to seek his fortune, of Lucy's forced inclusion in the harem of Enoch Drebber, and of her death shortly afterward of a broken heart. Holmes' eyes narrowed and his voice tensed as he described Jefferson Hope returning to find his sweetheart dead. Then, in a whisper he told his captive audience of Hope stealing into the room where her corpse was laid out and removing the wedding ring, which he carried ever after as a goad to his rage as he pursued Drebber from city to city and finally to London to seek revenge.

Once started, Holmes told this tale with his eyes focused in the distance and as if his two listeners weren't in the room with him; it was a compulsive repetition of a delusion that had haunted him for weeks.

When he finished he found two men looking

up at him, neither knowing what to say. Then Gregson began to ask the question which naturally came to his mind. "Very interesting, Mr. Holmes, but how do you know . . . "

Watson cut in, "Yes, I would also like to know how it is that you can choose, out of all these details, the ones which must be the important clues? You make it seem so . . . so elementary."

"Elementary? If you say so, my dear fellow."

Next morning, 6th. March

John Watson arose early, hoping to be the first one to bring in the morning paper, *The Echo,* from the hall table where the landlady left it. He was anxious to get to the paper before Holmes in order to see if the bogus article had been successfully included. He was surprised, however, to see that Sherlock was already up and seated at the breakfast table in his velvet dressing gown with the paper open before him. With trepidation Watson took his seat opposite Holmes, holding his breath.

"Ah, Watson, you'll find this good reading," Holmes said, handing over the open paper and pointing to an article.

Watson turned the page toward the light from the window next to him.

"The public," the article began, "has lost a sensational treat through the sudden death of the man Jefferson Hope ... "

"What's that?" Watson gasped. "Dead? Jefferson Hope dead?"

"Read on," said Holmes.

" ... death of the man Jefferson Hope, who was suspected of the murder of Mr. Enoch Drebber and Mr. Joseph Stangerson. The details of the case will probably never be known now, though we are informed upon good authority that the crime was the result of an old-standing and romantic feud, in which love and Mormonism bore a part. It seems that both the victims belonged in their youth to the Latter Day Saints and Hope, the deceased prisoner, hails also from the American West. If the case has had no other effect, it at least brings out in the most striking manner the efficiency of our detective police force, and will serve as a lesson to all foreigners that they will do wisely to settle their feuds at home, and not to carry them onto British soil. It is an open secret that the credit of this smart capture belongs to the well-known Scotland

Yard officials, Messrs. Lestrade and Gregson. The man was apprehended, it appears, in the rooms of a certain Mr. Sherlock Holmes, who has himself, as an amateur, shown some talent in the detective line, and who, with such instructors, may hope in time to attain some degree of their skills. It is expected that a testimonial of some sort will be presented to the two officers as a fitting recognition of their service."

Watson looked up from the paper into Sherlock Holmes's ironic smile.

"Didn't I tell you so when we started?" he said. "That's the result of our Study in Scarlet."

"Never mind," Watson answered, "I have all the true facts in my journal. When it is published, the public shall know them."

"Ah, my innocent friend, were it so simple. The case of Jefferson Hope is but a piece of the puzzle. It is after all only part of his game with me. A game which must end some day, as in chess, off in one far corner of the board."

"Beg your pardon?"

Watson was staring at his companion with an open mouth.

"It's all right there in the article, my dear Watson. Surely you spotted it. He has made it plain."

It was then that Watson glanced again at the page and saw what his eyes, at first, had passed over. Sherlock had underlined some of the letters with a pencil: the M, O and R in "Mormonism," the I in "It," the A, R and T in "part" and the Y in "youth". Put together the letters spelled, "moriarty"—meaningless to Watson. He was baffled.

"It's all here, you say?"

Holmes stared at Watson hard for a moment and seemed about to say more, then abruptly got up.

"This business with the police has kept me from the laboratory for days now." He was on his way to his room when he stopped suddenly as if struck by a thought and mumbled to himself, "Wait! Perhaps that was his aim, to keep me from my experiments." He smiled and then began to chuckle. "Yes, I see it now. Certainly that was his aim. Yes, yes there is no doubt." He laughed outright. "High marks for you, Professor!"

Back fully in the present, he spoke to Watson in a cheerful voice, "I may be late for dinner, Doctor. Don't wait for me."

Monday, 14th. March

March was living up to its reputation and

lashing the windows with icy rain. The smoke from Mycroft's cigar floated upward against the inside of the windowpane. He was smiling and feeling very content to be in the warm office with its crackling fire, and listening to his visitors' happy recounting of the charade they had just brought to a successful end.

"I'll tell you, Brandon Neal," John Watson said jovially, "you went too far. I only said to give the credit to the inspectors. You crowned them with laurels and built monuments to them."

"I know, I know," I replied. "I couldn't hold Lestrade back once he got the bit in his mouth."

Watson said, "I was startled to read of the death of Jefferson Hope, that is, James Brock. Not knowing beforehand of his death, by the way, allowed me to react most genuinely. I might otherwise have betrayed myself."

Mycroft turned around from the window to face John and me seated in easy chairs before the fire.

"My friends, I have been privy to some very cunning diplomatic schemes, skillfully executed. But your performance deserves bouquets of roses. You wouldn't by chance be interested in doing some undercover work for the Ministry?"

Good-humored chuckling followed his offer, as he went to each man to refill his glass with Scotch whisky.

He took a chair himself and became serious.

"I owe you gentlemen my deepest gratitude for your efforts, and also that friend of yours in Vienna for his sincere advice for I have good to report to you. The first is that Sherlock, while not asking yet to take over the management of his finances, has dispensed with the code in the book routine. He asked me straight out two days ago for his envelope of money. Also, I'm sure he has not been spying around the Ministry. From what I just heard Dr. Watson report, his mood has not been 'labile'—to use the good doctor's term—nor has he any of the signs of using drugs or adopting disguises. So, it appears to me that the program has been totally successful."

I considered both what I had just been told and also the optimism of Sherlock's brother. I knew I had to qualify that optimism, but I hesitated to take away another's joy.

"I can see that you do not wholly agree with my assessment," Mycroft prodded, looking at me.

"You're quite right, Mr. Holmes, the program has brought about the containment we wished for, but I must warn you that a relapse is always a possibility in cases such as this. I'm afraid it will be a matter of constant vigilance for ominous signs."

"You will continue to be there with him, won't

you, Doctor Watson?" Worry was evident in Mycroft's tone.

"I have no other plans at present, and he is an interesting person to share lodgings with," Watson answered.

"I'm relieved to hear that."

"Also, Lestrade and Gregson so enjoyed the little adventure that I'm sure they are ready to find another suitable case for Sherlock to solve," I said.

"A possible problem just came to mind," Watson put in. "With the publication of this case, might it be likely that members of the public, having read of his superior powers of deduction, would seek his help on their own. If that happens, we will have less control and management of the affair."

"Yes," replied Mycroft. "Dr. Watson is right. We must do something to head off that eventuality. Perhaps we could employ someone other than Lestrade or Gregson to approach Sherlock for help on the next case, an actor perhaps."

"Excellent idea," I said with enthusiasm. "If the *public* is seeking his services it would have the effect of strengthening his self-image as a great consulting detective."

Watson turned to me. "Your mention of a

possible relapse a moment ago reminds me of an incident that occurred right after I finished reading the newspaper article in the *Echo*. I had just assured Sherlock that I was going to write the account that would set the facts straight as to whom the credit belonged, when he began talking about it not being that simple and then made reference to some kind of game someone was playing with him. He could see that I plainly didn't understand what he was talking about and directed my attention to the article again. I saw then that he had underlined some letters with a pencil. I still didn't understand and I think I asked him what it meant. He looked . . . furtive, secretive and announcing that he had work to do in the laboratory, left."

"Hmm, I don't like the sound of this," I said. "Do you remember the letters he underlined?"

"No, but I tore out the piece from the paper." He reached into his inside coat pocket. "Here it is."

I took the piece of newsprint and noticed the underlined letters. "M,O,R,I,A,R,T,Y," I read.

"Someone's name? Moriarty?" Mycroft speculated.

"Could be. Maybe this is the person who is playing this game with him," I ventured.

"Yes, he called him, 'Professor,'" Watson added.

"Now I remember the other part. He said it was a game that would have to end, as in chess, on a far corner of the board."

"Interesting," I said "But no more than one should expect. It is typical of the psychotically paranoid to hold a deep, central paranoid delusion. And it is also typical when they are directly questioned about it to close up, as if the questioner is trying to steal the delusion from them. No, that's not well stated. It's as if the delusion is precious—all their own—and anyone learning the details would destroy it. Gentlemen, I'm afraid we're going to hear more about this Moriarty."

Mycroft Holmes was a man who was accustomed to problems only being solved for the time being. He was satisfied to have a success however temporary it might be. He raised his glass.

"To our victory on the field today then. Only the gods know who will win the war."

When the sip of Scotch symbolizing victory had been swallowed by all, Mycroft said in a conspiratorial tone, "One thing else about which I'd be pleased to hear your honest opinion."

"What is that?" I asked.

"Mr. Brock, the estate agent, claimed he was interrupted in the course of looking for the money he believed Stangerson to have in his room. He further claimed that he left the room and descended the ladder immediately after Stangerson's accidental stabbing. In other words, he didn't find any money. There must have been money, however, for Drebber to have been able to close the deal that night. Either it was on his person, or it was in the possession of his secretary. Brock denied finding any and the police found none. The Home Secretary and I had a discussion about whether Brock's account was true, or if instead Brock found the money and it now lies deep within a household hidey-hole in the Brock residence. Have you gentlemen considered this possibility?"

I looked over at John. On our blank faces Mycroft Holmes could read the answer to his question. "Very well then, what are your thoughts now?"

I shrugged. "Of course, I don't know. I'm pretty sure that neither Lestrade nor Gregson has considered this question either. Although they have proved their consummate acting skills, there would have been no need for them to prevaricate in our presence. Indeed, I believe they would have enjoyed showing their understanding of the criminal mind."

"That is also the opinion of the Home Secretary and myself. I'll tell you what he said to me. 'Mycroft, it is a matter of who should have the money—Drebber's heirs or Brock's family. If the Brock house was searched and the money was found, it should *legally* make the voyage back to America, but without doubt it is more needed in the Brock coffers. And, isn't there something about possession being nine points of the law?'"

Laughing, Watson raised his glass again. "Gentlemen, a toast to the Home Secretary."

John and I left Mycroft's office through the secret panel and the stairs into the tunnel beneath the Ministry. We got into a four-wheel cab at the back entrance of the adjacent building and immediately pulled the side-curtains closed. Watson was riding as far as a side street off Wigmore Street where he would get another cab to Baker Street, thus arriving alone.

The rain pelted the cab's thin roof. I raised my voice to be heard. "I didn't want to say it to Mr. Holmes back there, John, but I'm worried about this Moriarty."

"Yes, I feel that too," Watson said.

"From what you just said back there—beyond the Mormon story—Sherlock is attributing the motive for the 'murders' to this Moriarty's wish to keep him from pursuing his 'experiments.' Talk about nar-cissism. All evil in the world becomes Moriarty's way of playing a game with Holmes."

"Not good, not good."

"On the other hand, isn't this what we have been aiming to achieve, to focus—condense—isolate his paranoia so that it will not break loose in a wild uncontrolled expansion to include everyone?"

"I see your point. Moriarty, serving as he seems to, shrinks the central delusion to one person rather than moving in the opposite direction. Moriarty may turn out be our ally. In the meantime, Brandon, I think we should press the Scotland Yarders to come up with another problem soon to keep him busy."

"I agree, John."

Mycroft's having mentioned my Viennese friend, Sigmund Freud, reminded me that I needed to write to him and convey Mycroft's thanks and also give him a detailed account of the effect of our therapeutic experiment.

We rode in silence for a few minutes before Watson spoke again. "You know there are a couple of things that have me stumped."

"What's that, John?"

"Brandon, why did the dog die? We know he didn't die, as Sherlock thinks, from poison in the second pill. So why did he die?"

"John, if there had been none of the business of giving the poor old creature pills, what would you say—as a medical man—was the most likely cause of death of an old and ailing dog?"

"Hmm, put like that, an old dog near death for days, I'd say he died of natural causes. He'd reached the end of a dog's three score and ten."

"Exactly. We were just dashed lucky that he chose that particular moment to leave us humans to our nonsense."

"Yes, I can see that's the answer. We were *very* lucky. I believe neither the two inspectors nor I breathed a breath during that whole demonstration with the pills."

"Here's another lucky coincidence," I said. "When the chemist asked me how many of the little pills I wanted him to make up, I answered 'two'. I don't know why I said 'two'. I could as easily have said 'one'. The two pills allowed Sherlock to come up with that splendid idea of the duel, a creative achievement that pleased him very much, don't you think?"

"Yes, and it should have pleased him. It was brilliant indeed, a moment of brilliance that saved our our whole project. But here's another thing that puzzles me."

I turned to look at my friend and smiled. "Saving them up for me, is that it? All right, let's have it."

"As you know, Sherlock claimed that his whole solution hinged upon the wedding ring that fell to the floor when Drebber's body was lifted. We know it wasn't the ring from the finger of a dead girl in Utah, so my friend, how did the ring come to be there?"

I thought about his question as the cab hurried, rocking along. In the end, I answered, "John, old man, I haven't the foggiest idea."

The End